PUPPET

EVA WISEMAN

PUPPET

A NOVEL

TUNDRA BOOKS

Published in Canada by Tundra Books,
75 Sherbourne Street, Toronto, Ontario M5A 2P9

Published in the United States by Tundra Books of Northern New York,
P.O. Box 1030, Plattsburgh, New York 12901

Library of Congress Control Number: 2008903020

Library and Archives Canada Cataloguing in Publication

Wiseman, Eva
Puppet / Eva Wiseman.

ISBN 978-0-88776-828-6

1. Blood accusation – Europe – Juvenile fiction. 2. Jews – Persecutions – Europe – Juvenile fiction. 3. Trials (Murder) – Europe – Juvenile fiction. I. Title.

PS8595.I814P86 2008   jC813'.54   C2008-902061-8

We acknowledge the financial support of the Government of Canada through the Book Publishing Industry Development Program (BPIDP) and that of the Government of Ontario through the Ontario Media Development Corporation's Ontario Book Initiative. We further acknowledge the support of the Canada Council for the Arts and the Ontario Arts Council for our publishing program.

Design: Scott Richardson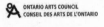
Typeset in Dante
Printed and bound in Canada

1 2 3 4 5 6   13 12 11 10 09

For my parents and my husband

—

"There is no witness so terrible, no accuser so powerful as the conscience which dwells within us."

SOPHOCLES (496 BC–406 BC)

ACKNOWLEDGMENTS

When I was a child and tattled on my younger sister, my mother would admonish me: "Don't be a Morris Scharf!" My curiosity was piqued. I asked her about the identity of Morris Scharf. My mother's recount of the blood accusation of Jewish people living in Tisza-Eszlar, Hungary, in 1882 and the blood libel court case that followed it in 1883 was the cornerstone of this novel. I based the trial scenes on the court transcripts from the *Egyetértés*, a daily Hungarian newspaper at the time, which were published in entirety in Elek Judit-Sükösd Mihály's 1990 book, *Tutajosok*.

I would like to thank my father, my husband, and my children for their critical reading of the manuscript of this book.

I also want to thank my editors Kathy Lowinger and Heather Sangster for never steering me wrong.

I want to express my appreciation to the Canada Council for the Arts and the Manitoba Arts Council for their support.

JULY 1876

THE VILLAGE OF TISZA-ESZLAR, HUNGARY

It happened a long time ago when we were young girls in short skirts. It was before my ma got sick and even before Esther's mother had to sell their cow, Magda.

In the field behind Esther's house, we were lying in the tall grass. It tickled the bottom of our bare feet. I was chewing on a blade of grass, luxuriating in the summer sunshine hot on our faces and legs and arms. Esther's eyes were closed. A happy smile on her face transformed her plain features to near prettiness.

Suddenly, her stomach growled so loudly I could hear it.

"I'm hungry!" she said.

I spat out the blade of grass. "Me too." I peered into the sky. "It's another hour to lunch."

It was useless to ask Esther's mother for food. The whole village knew Widow Solymosi had trouble enough scraping together the daily meals of four hungry people.

Esther pushed herself up onto her elbows.

"I'm starving! I can't wait another minute to eat something."

"Well, you'll have to, unless you want to eat grass like Magda."

She laughed. "I won't eat grass, but you gave me an idea. I'll milk Magda. The milk will tide us over."

I sat up.

"You can't! You don't know how and you're too young. Your mama will never let you milk the cow."

"She doesn't have to find out. I know what to do. I've seen her do it a thousand times."

She stood up and pulled me off the ground.

"You'll get in trouble," I warned her.

"You're such a scaredy-cat, Julie. Mama will never find out. She's helping Farmer Veres in the fields today. She won't be home till nightfall."

Magda was lying on the straw in the barn. She struggled to her feet when she saw us. Esther undid the latch on the gate and we went into the cow's stall. She scratched Magda behind her ear. The cow mooed.

"See how friendly she is?"

Esther slapped Magda's flank. The cow mooed again.

Then she took a milking stool and bucket from the corner of the stall. Placing the stool beside the cow's rump, she lined up the pail under her udder and grabbed one of the cow's teats. I retreated to the farthest corner of the stall.

"Don't be such a coward," she said. "Watch me."

She squeezed the cow's teat, but no milk came out.

"I guess I'm not squeezing hard enough."

"Stop it!" I pleaded.

Magda looked so big and I was afraid she would trample me. I tried to take another step back but couldn't. The rough wooden walls of the stall felt scratchy against my neck and my arms.

"I'm going to squeeze harder." I saw Esther's hands move, and a second later Magda's hind hooves flew into the air. Esther fell back, the stool on its side, as her pail clattered to the floor. Magda took a step. Esther screamed.

"My foot! My foot! Help me!"

I ran at the cow, butting my head against her rump, pushing her away from Esther with my arms. The cow wouldn't budge. Esther was bleating with pain.

The stool was upended on the floor. I picked it up and threw it at Magda's hindquarters with all my might. She finally lumbered off Esther's right foot.

I dragged Esther out of the barn, a trail of blood marking our way. I laid her down on the ground. Her eyes were closed and she was white as snow. When I saw the large, open wound at the base of her big toe, I ran to get help.

CHAPTER I

FRIDAY, MARCH 17, 1882

Leslie the Brave grasped the handle of the frying pan and held it high in the air, ready to smite the black-hearted Devil cowering at his feet.

"This will teach you not to ravish young maidens!" cried Leslie as his frying pan met the top of the Devil's noggin with a loud thunk.

The audience's cheers almost drowned out Leslie's words. He bowed in our direction, and the Devil sprang to his feet and ran away. As soon as Leslie noticed he had lost his quarry, he was in hot pursuit.

Sophie Solymosi and I were standing so close to the stage that I could see every crack on Leslie the Brave's wooden face, his bulbous red nose, and the stains on the puppet's braided scarlet coat.

I looked for Esther among the laughing villagers, but

there was no sign of her. She had promised her sister and me that she would try to get her mistress's permission to come. After all, traveling puppet shows were a rare occurrence in remote Tisza-Eszlar.

"Do you see Esther anywhere?" Sophie's broad face was full of concern. "She should be here by now."

"I guess Mrs. Huri wouldn't let her come."

"That witch treats my little sister worse than a slave! Mama says that the minute we have two forints to rub together, Esther will be able to quit."

We turned back to the stage. Leslie the Brave was tip-toeing behind the Devil's back, his frying pan once again high in the air. A child's high-pitched voice rose from the back of the crowd.

"What's Leslie the Brave doing?" he asked.

He was shushed by an older boy, about my age, holding his hand. I recognized him right away. It was Morris Scharf, with his little brother, Sam. Their black pants, the tassels hanging out from below their white shirts, and the black skull caps covering their hair marked them as Jew boys from the Old Village. They stood out like ravens among the peasant women in their embroidered skirts and many petticoats and the men in their wide pantaloons. The long, curling forelocks in front of their ears made them seem strange and exotic. Morris was much taller and skinnier than I remembered.

I watched him, curious, for I hadn't talked to Morris in a long time. He and I were the same age. We used to play together when we were young children while my ma sewed for Mrs. Rosenberg, a friend of Morris's stepmother. Morris could barely speak Hungarian, but it didn't matter. We played wild games of tag among the rose bushes in Mrs. Rosenberg's garden while Ma was fitting her for her new clothes. When I grew older, Ma left me at home when she went to her fine ladies' houses. The rare times I saw Morris in the streets, he would say a bashful hello but hurry off before I could speak to him. Jew boys kept to themselves.

I must have been staring because Morris glanced up and our eyes met for a moment. He lowered his head and a crimson flush crept into his cheeks. I had to bite my lip to stop myself from laughing. He looked so funny with his ears on fire.

I turned back to the stage when the crowd around us began to scream and whistle. They began to chant "Kill the Devil! Kill the Devil!" Leslie the Brave knocked the Devil to the ground and was sitting on top of him, bringing the play to an end.

"That was funny!" I said to Sophie as I adjusted my kerchief to make sure it covered my left cheek.

Sophie slipped her arm through mine. "Let's go home."

"Do you want to stop off at Mrs. Huri's to see Esther?"

"That old crow won't let Esther talk to us," said Sophie glumly.

"We can try speaking to her in the yard, while Mrs. Huri is inside. I'm worried about Esther."

Sophie sighed. "So am I. She's been acting strange lately. She never smiles. She's always so sad. Remember how she used to sing like a songbird while she worked? She never opens her mouth nowadays, and she won't tell me what's bothering her when I ask her."

"Perhaps she'll tell me."

As we picked our way through the audience, I looked for the Jew boys, but they had disappeared.

We snuck into Mrs. Huri's yard through the side gate. Esther was feeding chickens grain from a wide wicker basket. There were large chickens and small chickens, fat chickens and a few puny ones. Bright yellow chicks at the back of the brood were desperately pecking at the ground. The squawking of the hungry birds was deafening. There was no sign of Esther's mistress.

She greeted us listlessly.

"Why didn't you come to the puppet show? We were waiting for you," said Sophie.

"Mrs. Huri wouldn't let me leave." Esther shrugged her shoulders. "I don't care."

She threw the last handful of feed among the chickens, put down the basket on the porch steps, and wiped her hands on her apron.

"I'm going to eat my lunch. Can you stay for a while?" she asked.

I didn't know what to do. If Pa got home before me, he'd have my hide. I studied the sun. With some luck, I had a few minutes of freedom left.

"Pa probably won't be home yet. I can stay."

"So can I," said Sophie.

Sophie worked as a maid for the Rosenbergs, who treated her as well as their daughter, Rosie. Her clothes were much nicer than Esther's and mine. She could come and go as she pleased, as long as her chores were done.

Esther led us down a narrow path that cut through a vegetable garden at the back of the yard. She unlatched a door set into the wooden fence and we walked toward the meandering stream almost obscured by the bulrushes on its banks. Esther pulled aside the tall, reedy plants to reveal a small clearing. Sophie and I squeezed through the bulrushes and sat down on the ground beside her.

"This is my secret place," she said. "I come here whenever I can. The mistress can't find me here."

She pulled a piece of dark bread out of her apron pocket.

"Do you want to share?" she asked.

The sight of the bread made my mouth water, but I shook my head. I knew that was all she was given for her meal.

"I'll eat at home."

"Me too," said Sophie.

"I'm not really hungry," said Esther and began to pick at the crust.

8

"I wish you could have seen the puppet show," said Sophie. "It was so funny! I couldn't stop laughing."

"Leslie the Brave makes a wonderful hero."

Esther didn't seem to be paying attention to us. Her arms were wound across her chest as she rocked back and forth, her eyes fixed on the gurgling clear waters below us. We could see the pebbles on the streambed and tiny silvery fish darting about.

"The water," said Esther in a dreamy voice. "It's so pure, so clean."

I had the feeling she had forgotten we were with her.

"What's the matter with you?" asked Sophie. "Talk to us!"

Esther blinked as if surprised back into wakefulness. She plucked at the red-striped belt she always wore around her waist.

"What's the use?" she asked. "Each day is the same as the day before, full of misery, hunger, backbreaking work. It'll never change." Her voice cracked and she wiped away a tear with a corner of her apron. "Sometimes, I think I should just . . ."

"Just what?" said Sophie. I shared the fear in her voice. "Just what?" she repeated. "Talk to me, Esther. What's the matter with you?"

Esther didn't reply for a long moment.

"I can't –"

A harsh voice from behind the fence interrupted her. We heard footsteps crunching on the grass.

9

"Where are you, Esther? Where are you, girl? I need you. Don't think you can hide from me!"

Esther put her finger to her lips and we fell silent. I was afraid even to breathe.

The footsteps receded. Esther pushed the bulrushes aside and peeked out.

"I have to get back to the house!"

In an instant, she had disappeared.

The spring sun warmed the crown of my head. It also reminded me that Pa would be home soon.

"I have to go too. Pa will want his lunch."

I didn't have to explain to Sophie why I was running. She knew my father.

Even during the brightest part of the day, the sun barely penetrated the narrow windows of our cottage. It took a few seconds before my eyes adjusted to the gloom and I could see the clay walls Ma had convinced Pa to whitewash. He had grumbled that it was a waste of money. I had to blink several times before I could make out the rough-hewn wooden table and chairs in the center of the room. The four cots lining the walls were the only other pieces of furniture. There was also a wood-burning metal fireplace in the corner that gave us heat in the winter. I had chopped wood, stacked it in the fireplace, and lit it before I left the house for the puppet show. I realized Pa would be angry that I made a fire on such a warm afternoon, but Ma was always so cold nowadays. Through an open door, I could see into the chimneyless kitchen with its cast-iron stove and door leading to the yard. When she was still able to cook, Ma had always left this door open to allow the smoke to escape.

Ma was lying on the cot closest to the fireplace. Clara was sitting on the clay floor, crooning softly to the doll I had made for her out of a stick of wood and some rags. I noticed how my sister's thin arms and legs stuck out from under her skirt and blouse. She was three years old and growing fast. I would have to get some money somehow to buy material for new clothes for her. On one of her good days, Ma would sew her a new dress in no time.

Ma's eyes were closed and I was glad she seemed to be asleep. Sleep was the only respite she got from the terrible pain gnawing at her. It was about a year ago that the pain first came. Ma tried to ignore it, but after a while it couldn't be ignored. She begged and cajoled Pa in her gentle way, but he wouldn't agree to call the Jew doctor to come and see her. He said that you couldn't trust one of them Jews.

The day came when I couldn't stand to see her suffer any longer. Pa was working in the fields, so I fetched Dr. Weltner myself. I knew Pa would beat me if he ever found out, but I didn't care.

When the doctor's horse-drawn buggy arrived, Ma told me to take Clara outside. I carried her to the yard, but I left the back door open a crack so I could hear what was going on inside. I set Clara down to play in the dirt and stole up to the door to listen.

No sound came from the room.

"Come here, Julie," Clara cried from behind me. "Look what I drawed!"

I rushed up to hush her.

"Look what I drawed!" she repeated, pointing to the stick figure she had traced in the dirt. "It's a princess!"

"She's beautiful, just like you. Draw another one."

I went back to the door. It was still silent in the room, then a bag was snapped closed.

"I am afraid that I have bad news for you, Mrs. Vamosi," the doctor said solemnly.

I crept even closer and nudged the door open a little more so I could see what was happening.

The doctor was sitting on Ma's bed, patting her hands.

"You have a tumor in your breast," he said.

I could hear the sudden intake of Ma's breath.

"I don't understand," she said, her voice quivering.

"It's cancer," the doctor said. "Something that shouldn't be there is growing inside your chest. I am afraid there is nothing I can do to help you. There is no cure for your disease."

A sob escaped Ma's lips. "Dear Mother of God, what will I do? What will happen to me? What will happen to my girls?"

"I might not be able to cure you, but I can give you something to help with the pain – at least for a while."

"We have no money for medicines."

"Don't worry about the money," the doctor said. He took something out of his bag and handed it to Ma. I couldn't see what it was. "When you can't bear the pain, fill a thimble with this powder, mix it with water, and drink it. It will help with the pain, although it will make you drowsy."

"My husband won't let me accept charity," Ma whispered.

"Trust me, Mrs. Vamosi. You will need the medicine. Hide it where your husband won't see it. It will help," he repeated.

Clara started crying. I ran to pick her up. By the time I had soothed her, the doctor was climbing back into his buggy.

I took Clara into the house. When I asked, Ma wouldn't tell me what the doctor had said to her. Nor was there a sign of the powder. However, I always knew when Ma took her medicine because she slurred her words and became sleepy. As the days went by, she took her medicine more and more often. I could also see by the tightening of her lips and her moans that it was helping her less and less with each passing day. My ma who used to love to sing, my ma who used to make better meals out of very little than anybody else, my ma who used to braid my hair, my ma who used her gentle ways to rein in Pa's temper – that Ma was forever gone. Nowadays, she spent her days in bed, dozing off, restlessly waking and then crying whenever her eyes rested on Clara or me.

I bent down and kissed the top of her head softly. She was burning up. I wet a rag with water from the earthenware pitcher on the table and tried to squeeze a few drops into her mouth. Then I dampened her face and hands gently with the cloth. The pitcher was half-empty. I would have to go to the village well tomorrow for drinking water while Clara took her nap.

Clara began to whine.

"I'm hungry, Julie. Give me something to eat."

There was only a little milk at the bottom of the pail. Pa would be angry if he didn't have milk with his meal, so I knew better than to give it to Clara. She would have to be satisfied with water. I poured water into a tin cup that had been patched several times by the traveling tinsmith. I cut a thick slice from the dark loaf of bread I had baked two days ago. There was still some lard left, so I spread it thickly on top. A large potato from yesterday's dinner completed the meal.

"I want milk! I hate water!" Clara grumbled, just as I knew she would.

She fell silent as the front door swung open and Pa came into the cottage. I quickly tightened my kerchief. Pa did not like to see his handiwork.

Pa glanced at Clara and me and, without a word, sat down at the table. He didn't look at Ma. Fortunately, there was still a chunk of bacon left. I put it on a tin plate, cut him a generous slice of bread, and poured the remainder of the

milk into a cup. I hated myself for the nervous way I scurried about, trying to please him. I stood beside the table,
careful to be out of reach of his fists, waiting for him to
notice me. The only noise in the room came from Ma's tor-
turous breathing.

When Pa continued to ignore me, I knew that I had to
speak up.

"Pa," I said, trying to steady the tremor in my voice. "Pa,
I'm sorry to ask you again, but I need some money. There
is no food in the house. Even the milk is gone. I should go
over to Mrs. Huri's."

We didn't have a cow of our own, so we had to buy our
milk from Mrs. Huri. She had two cows.

Pa's fingers tightened around the cup. I stepped back. I
couldn't help it – my hand snuck up to my left cheek, but
my kerchief was still covering the dark bruise. He had hit
me a few days ago when I asked him for money for food.

He grunted, reached into his pocket, and threw a handful
of coins on the table. I couldn't believe my luck. There was
enough here for milk, a whole slab of bacon, and even
some money left over for material for Clara. I put the coins
in my pocket with a trembling hand before he could change
his mind.

"Thank you, Pa," I stammered.

"I had some work this morning," he said in a gruff voice.
"Rosenberg needed help on his farm. That dirty Jew, he has
so much money he doesn't know what to do with it. Those

15

people steal money out of the pockets of God-fearing Christian men."

He slammed his palm down on the table so violently his plate and cup jumped. I remained silent. I knew from experience he would become even angrier if I spoke.

"Rosenberg barely noticed whether I was doing what he paid me for. He was excited about the new butcher they're hiring. It's got to be somebody who can do all their crazy rituals. Can you imagine, they want somebody who'll kill their cows and chickens according to their Jew laws, and sing prayers on their Sabbath too." He snorted.

Clara began to croon to her doll.

"Shut your mouth!" Pa snapped. "Stop that caterwauling!"

He jumped up, his hand raised high. Clara began to cry. I stood in front of her, my arms spread wide to shield her.

"Stop it, Peter! Leave the girls alone! They've done nothing wrong," called Ma weakly.

He hesitated, lowered his arm, and, turning on his heels, stomped out of the cottage.

"Bitch!" he muttered under his breath as he slammed the door behind him.

Clara and I ran to Ma's bed and fell on our knees beside it.

"Ma! Ma!" Clara cried. "You're awake, Ma!"

Ma patted her on the cheek. She motioned for me to lean closer.

"Your pa . . ." she whispered, "your pa has a lot on his mind. That's why . . ."

"He is a bully, Ma! A real bully!"

"You mustn't say that . . . He is your pa. You must respect your pa!"

"But Ma . . ."

I never finished my sentence. She closed her eyes and returned to oblivion.

I was hanging laundry on the clothesline in the yard when I heard somebody clearing his throat behind me. I turned around and dropped the shirt I was holding when I saw who it was. Morris Scharf was shifting from foot to foot, a covered tin pot in his hands.

"Hello, Julie." He held the pot toward me. "My step-mama hear your mama sick. She made her soup."

"Pardon?" I could barely understand what he was saying through his heavy accent. He tried again.

"I hope your mama feel better." I didn't want to ask him to repeat the words that were obviously kind, but I couldn't help myself. "Your Hungarian, why is it so odd?"

"My papa wife not my real mama. She teach my brother, Sam, but she don't care about me."

"And your papa?"

"Papa Hungarian good, but he too busy to teach me. But we study Torah together," he said proudly.

"Would you like to sit for a moment?"

"I cannot. New sochet, new butcher hire. I go hear."

I thought I had managed the thick fog of his accent, but I still did not understand what he was saying. "Do all of your priests kill animals?"

He shook his head. "No. In small village we can afford only one person who knows rituals. So butcher priest."

He mystified me. I thanked him with a smile and took the pot of fragrant soup gratefully.

CHAPTER 2

SATURDAY, APRIL 1, 1882

The memory of winter was still in the air as I made my way to Mrs. Huri's house in the New Village. I was glad of Ma's shawl around my shoulders, but the ground was cold under my bare feet. I wished I was still wearing my boots, but to spare the leather we always took them off on the first day of April and wouldn't wear them again until fall. The earthenware jug I was balancing on my hip was heavy even though it was empty.

The streets were coming alive on this bright Saturday morning. Merchants were opening their shops. A man with a donkey cart was delivering lumber.

I finally arrived at Mrs. Huri's house. It was much larger than our cottage and much nicer with its thatched roof and walls painted a cheerful yellow. I knocked on the front door, but there was no answer. I knew somebody was home by the yelling going on inside, but I couldn't make out what was being said. I shifted the jug to my other hip and rapped on the door more loudly. Still no answer. Finally, I turned the doorknob and the door swung open.

I stood on the threshold, rooted in my tracks. The room was completely empty except for a few paintbrushes, brooms, and dustpans. I could see through an open door on the far wall that the furniture had been piled up in the courtyard. The stuffing that had been taken out of the straw mattresses was blowing about in the breeze.

Mrs. Huri was chasing Esther around the empty room, swishing a long and supple stick at her. Mrs. Huri's little son and daughter were huddled in a corner, crying.

"This'll teach you to be such a lazy, good-for-nothing girl!" said Mrs. Huri with another wave of her stick. Her handsome face was contorted by anger. "You don't listen to me! Didn't I tell you to get everything ready for spring cleaning?"

"You surely did, mistress!" cried Esther. "I'm so sorry, but I didn't know you wanted to paint the bottom half of the walls today. They looked clean to me."

Mrs. Huri raised her stick.

"How dare you question my orders!" she snarled.

"I don't, mistress! I never do!" said Esther. She sunk to the floor, covering her head with her hands. "Please don't hit me! I'll go to the store to buy the blue paint if you want me to."

Mrs. Huri lowered the stick.

"Of course you'll go. The Jew store in the New Village will be closed today. You'll have to get it at Kohlmayer's in the Old Village. And you better be quick about it!" she added with another swish of her stick.

When she noticed me, her complexion darkened.

"What are you doing here, spying on me?" she roared. "How dare you sneak up on me?"

I kept my voice level.

"I'm sorry, mistress. The door was open. You didn't hear me when I knocked."

"What do you want?"

"My pa was wondering if you could sell us some milk?"

I held out my money. She grabbed the coins greedily.

"My milk is in great demand, but your pa is an old customer," she said curtly. "Esther, fill up her jug with the milk in the kitchen!"

"But, mistress, the milk in the kitchen is from yesterday. Let me milk the cow. It'll take only a few minutes and then I'll be able to give Julie fresh milk."

Esther was speaking so meekly I could barely hear her.

Mrs. Huri's fingers tightened on the handle of her stick.

"You insolent girl! How dare you question my orders?" She looked like one of her angry hens. "You'll do exactly as you're told!"

"The milk from the kitchen will be fine," I said quickly.

I didn't want Esther punished because of me. I followed her into the kitchen and she filled up my jug from a pail full of milk.

"I'm sorry," she whispered. "She is too mean to give you fresh milk."

"It'll be gone before it has a chance to curdle."

After she filled my jug, Esther lifted the pail and drank greedily from it.

"The mistress gave me no food for breakfast," she said, "not even a cup of milk. She said we were too busy cleaning to eat. I'm so hungry!"

Mrs. Huri came into the kitchen.

"You're still here? Be gone with you," she yelled. "Stop wasting my girl's time!"

"Meet me by the well. I'll wait for you," I whispered to Esther behind her mistress's back before I scurried out of the house.

The well was in the village square, across the street from the Jew church, an ugly, squat building that didn't look like a church at all. It had no spires or bells like the churches Esther and I attended every Sunday. I waited for Esther for the best part of a half-hour. Several women were lined up at the well, filling their containers with drinking water. The water from the wells in our own yards was fit only for animals.

By the time Esther got there, the sun was shining weakly. I judged that it must have been an hour before noon. Esther finally saw me waving at her. She had on an unbuttoned red, white, and black plaid jacket, white blouse, black skirt, and white apron. The red-striped belt she always wore was twisted around her waist and she was barefoot like me. She was shivering despite the faded red shawl she had thrown over her shoulders. She was clutching a small tin container.

"Brrr, it's cold today. What I wouldn't give for my boots," she said miserably. "But the mistress says I have to save them for the fall and winter."

"Pa says that too. I'll keep you company. I don't have to go home yet. I'll come with you to get the paint at Kohlmayer's."

A strange look I couldn't identify flitted across her face. It was gone so quickly I thought I must have imagined it.

"Don't come," she said. "I must hurry or the mistress will skin me alive." She held out the container. "I don't have time to tarry. The mistress wants me to buy blue paint. Take the milk home to your ma and to Clara. They must be waiting for it."

"When will I see you? I wish you could get some time off. Ma and Clara would be so happy to visit with you. Pa is hardly ever home during the day."

"You know I'd love to come, but the mistress never lets me off except for church. All she does is yell and scream at me. Yesterday she was mad because I washed the dishes in the bread trough. Today – well, you heard why she was yelling today." Tears filled her eyes. "Sometimes I wonder if it wouldn't be better if . . ."

Her voice trailed off as we watched a group of men file into the Jew church. Morris and Sam walked hand in hand behind their father. Four Jew beggars followed them all into the building. I waved at Morris, but he didn't wave back.

I told Esther Pa's news about the butcher the Jews were hiring, but I could see she wasn't listening.

"I really have to go, Julie," she said. "The mistress will be mad if I don't get back quickly and Kohlmayer's is so far away."

Two old women at the fountain barred her path.

"I couldn't help overhearing that you're going to Kohlmayer's, dear," said Mrs. Lanczi, one of Mrs. Huri's neighbors. She patted Esther on the shoulder and pressed some money into Esther's hand. "Could you bring back a block of soap for me?"

"And bring me a few nails," added Mrs. Csordas. "I must fix the sole of my boots." She handed Esther a coin and stuck her hairy chin into her face. "Now be careful with my money!"

"I will," answered Esther. "I have to go, Julie!"

She broke into a run but then turned around and came back and hugged me.

"Good-bye, Julie! You're a good friend. The only friend I have."

Then with a final wave, she was gone. I never saw her again.

Ma was in a heavy sleep and I had just put Clara down for her nap. Pa was at the Rosenbergs' farm, and I was peeling potatoes in the kitchen for our evening meal. I tried to pare the skin so it would come off in one piece. I would take the potato skins with me the next time I went to see Sophie and Esther. We liked to throw the skins to the ground to see if they would fall in the shape of a letter. Mrs. Rosenberg had taught Sophie how to read, so she could tell us what letters the potato peels formed. If the letter matched the initial of a boy we knew, it meant we were fated to marry.

Suddenly, there was loud knocking on the door. I hastened to open it because I didn't want Clara to wake up.

Esther's mother stood in the yard. I stepped outside and closed the door behind me.

"Good day, Mrs. Solymosi! What brings you here?"

She was pale and on the verge of tears.

"Is my Esther here?" she asked in a shaky voice.

"I haven't seen her since this morning."

"Mrs. Huri told me you were at her house to buy milk. I was hoping Esther had come to visit you."

"I saw Esther at the well before she left for Kohlmayer's, but I haven't seen her since."

I sat down on the back steps and motioned for Mrs. Solymosi to join me, but she remained on her feet.

"Esther should have been back hours ago. Sophie and Rosie Rosenberg met her when she was heading back to Mrs. Huri's around one o'clock this afternoon, but she never arrived there. Mrs. Huri came to me looking for her. I've just been to Kohlmayer's, but he told me she had left his shop before noon. Where could she be?" She finally sank down onto the step beside me, her fingers working the tassels on her shawl. "It's not like Esther to go somewhere without telling her mistress. Esther is a good girl. A hard worker. If she didn't go back to Mrs. Huri's, something must have happened to her!"

She began to weep. I put my arms around her shoulders.

"My Esther must be hurt! I can feel it in my bones," she cried.

I didn't know what to say.

She struggled to her feet. "I'll go down to the riverbank. Esther might have gone there."

I remembered the depth of Esther's unhappiness the last time I saw her. I wondered what she had been about to tell me when the sight of the Jews distracted her. Surely she wouldn't . . . I pushed the thought out of my mind and told myself not to be stupid. I stood up.

"I'll come with you," I said.

Mrs. Huri was on her way home when we met her.

"I was at the Tisza," she said. "I remembered how much Esther loved the river so I thought she may have gone for a walk beside it." The hardness of her eyes was at war with the syrupy sweetness of her words. "I must go home now. My little ones will be waiting for me. If you find the dear child, tell her not to be late for supper."

Mrs. Solymosi stared after her.

"She is a hard woman, that one, no matter how she pretends to be so good and kind," she said. "Esther told me how badly she treats her. I am keeping my eyes open for another place for her." She began to weep again. "I wish Esther could give up her job with Mrs. Huri right away, but with Mr. Solymosi gone" – she crossed herself – "I can't feed four people. Esther will have to stay where she is. I'm lucky that both Sophie and Janos have good places."

As usual, the river was full of caravans of rafts transporting all kinds of goods – lumber, rock salt, and even fruits and vegetables.

Mrs. Solymosi scanned the riverbank.

"There is no sign of Esther anywhere! Where is my daughter?" she asked in a pathetic voice.

"Let's walk along the river." I grasped her hand. "Mrs. Huri might be right. Esther may have decided to take the day off and go for a stroll by the river."

I knew this was unlikely. Esther had seemed determined to return to Mrs. Huri's as quickly as possible, but I didn't want to upset Mrs. Solymosi further.

We walked along the Tisza, the same route Esther might have taken, but we did not see her. Finally, darkness fell and we had to return to our homes.

We said good-bye when we reached my cottage.

"I'm sure Esther will be waiting for you at home," I told Mrs. Solymosi.

We both knew how afraid Esther was of the dark.

CHAPTER 3

SUNDAY, APRIL 2, 1882

Esther kept invading my dreams that night. She was hovering above the Tisza River, her dress made of clouds and her feet clad in shiny red boots. Her face was serene and her lips were parted in a gentle smile. I called to her.

"Esther, where are you? Your mother is looking for you. Come home!"

"I am home."

She disappeared behind a cloud, and I woke up, more tired than when I had lowered my head to my pillow. Ma was snoring gently, and Clara was sucking her thumb in her sleep. Pa's bed was empty. He was always up before daylight, gone to Mr. Rosenberg's fields. Pa worked even on Sundays.

I dragged myself out of bed and washed my hands and face in the trough in the kitchen. I fed the chickens and geese and drew water from the well for them. I collected the eggs the hens had laid and put them in a tin bowl on a shelf in the kitchen. I would sell them in town later.

I was happy that I had milk for Clara's breakfast. It was time to wake both her and Ma.

I carried Clara to the outhouse despite her bitter complaints. She was good-natured but never first thing in the morning. As I held her in my arms, I noticed how light she was for a three-year-old. I decided to cut another slice of bread for her breakfast, even though Pa got mad when the loaf was eaten up too quickly.

When we returned to the house, Clara fell on her food like a hungry puppy.

Next, it was Ma's turn. I kissed her cheek. Her face was hot against my lips. Her eyes fluttered.

"Good morning, my daughter," she said with her sweet smile.

I propped her up against her pillow. Mornings were her best times. Sometimes she was even able to drink some milk.

Clara finished her breakfast and I settled her down on the floor to play with her doll. I sat at the foot of Ma's bed, like I did every morning, for our daily talk.

Ma glanced around the room.

"It's so nice and clean. Has a little angel come to our home to clean it up while I was sleeping?" she teased me. "Julie, my love, I am thirsty," she said. "Please give me a little water."

I poured milk into a tankard and gave it to her.

"There you go, Ma," I said. "The milk'll make you brawny again."

"You mean that I should drink the milk, Julie, because it'll make me strong again," Ma corrected me gently.

Ma used to be a seamstress for fine ladies before she got sick and she learned how to speak properly from them. She wanted me to be well spoken, like the ladies whose clothes she used to sew. "It will open doors for you, my girl." Her dreams for me seemed to make her happy.

Ma's workbox with its neat rows of different-colored yarns, needles, thimbles, and the sweetest little scissors occupied a place of honor on the floor next to her bed. From time to time, she would ask me to give her the box and she would run her fingers over its contents with a wistful look on her face.

"I'll be sewing again for my ladies before you know it," she'd always tell me as she snapped the lid closed.

"You will, Ma! You will!"

From the time I was a little girl, she taught me how to sew a straight seam and to patch a torn sleeve with stitches so tiny you could barely see them.

"You'll be a fine seamstress someday," she always promised me. "When I'm feeling better, I'll teach you all I know now that you're old enough. And when I save a little money, we'll apprentice you to a dressmaker in Budapest." I knew that we'd never have enough money and that Pa would never agree to such a plan. But I never contradicted her.

She refused to drink the milk and passed me the tankard.

"It's water I need," she said. "Save the milk for yourself and for Clara. Your pa likes his milk too."

There was no convincing her. I could see by the whiteness of her lips that her pain had returned. I got off the bed and filled a tin cup with the water left in the bottom of the jug and gave it to her. As I swept the floor I pretended not to notice that she pulled out a small packet and a thimble from beneath her pillow. She dipped the thimble into the packet and then dumped the white powder from it into the water. She drank the liquid down greedily.

A few minutes later, she called to me.

"I am feeling stronger. Today is going to be one of my good days. I just know it!"

I had been afraid to share the village news, but now the words tumbled out of my mouth.

"You won't believe what happened, Ma. Esther has disappeared! I just hope that nothing bad has happened to her."

"What do you mean disappeared?" Ma asked.

"Nobody has seen her since she left for Kohlmayer's on an errand for Mrs. Huri. She was so sad the last time I saw her. I am scared for her."

"That poor child!" Ma said. "I just hope she hasn't done anything foolish."

"What do you mean, Ma?"

She sighed.

"It's just that unhappy people sometimes . . ."

Her voice trailed off and her eyes closed. I shook her hands.

"Wake up, Ma! Don't sleep! What were you going to say?"

She didn't reply. I could tell by the shallowness of her breathing that she was fast asleep. I put her hands on top of her blanket and patted them. When I straightened up, I was startled to find Clara standing next to me.

"Why is Ma always sleeping?" she asked. "Why doesn't she ever do anything?"

"Hush your mouth. Don't talk like that about Ma. Can't you see she's sick? That's why she sleeps so much and can't do the things she used to." I took a deep breath. Ma was always telling me to be more patient with Clara. "Don't you remember what it was like before Ma got sick?" I asked. "Don't you remember how good Ma's cooking used to be? How much she used to laugh?"

Clara shook her head and began to bawl.

I picked her up and rubbed her back. I cut a crust from the bread in the kitchen and gave it to her.

"You can eat this if you promise to be a good girl. I have to go to the village well now. I'll be back in time for church."

I gave Clara her doll again. She was happily gnawing on the bread and cradling her baby in her arms when I left the house.

—

CHAPTER 4

SUNDAY, APRIL 2, 1882

Esther's mother was the first person I saw at the well. I waved to her, but she didn't notice me. She was busy talking to the women gathered around her. I could see the women shake their heads. When she finally saw me, she rushed to me, wild-eyed, the scarf on her head askew.

"She is still missing! She hasn't come home and nobody has seen her! Dear Lord! Where could my girl be?"

Three or four Jewish men were crossing the square to their church. One of them separated himself from the others and approached us. Behind him was Morris, holding Sam's hand. The boys were dressed in their usual black and white, and the man wore a long black coat and a black hat. His clothing gave him a forbidding air, but his expression was kind.

"Mrs. Solymosi," he said. "I'm so sorry for your troubles."

"Do I know you?" she asked angrily.

"I am Joseph Scharf, the shamash – I mean, the beadle in the synagogue." His Hungarian was perfect, but he spoke it with a strong foreign accent. "These are my sons, Morris and Sam." The boys remained silent.

"Hello, Morris, Sam," I said.

Morris nodded but wouldn't meet my gaze.

Esther's mother recoiled from them. She bumped into me and I must have made some kind of noise for the man's eyes shifted to my face. He must have read by my expression that I didn't understand him. "By synagogue, I mean our temple," he said, pointing at the building. "I am the shamash, the caretaker. My job is to keep the synagogue in good order."

He turned his attention back to Esther's mother.

"I decided to speak to you, Mrs. Solymosi, because I heard your daughter is missing. I know how worried you must be, for I have two sons." He smiled at the boys and patted the little one on the head. His younger son tugged at his trouser leg and Mr. Scharf scooped him up into his arms. Morris was drawing circles in the dirt with the toe of his boot. I saw him glance at my bare feet and then look away. Mr. Scharf spoke again.

"Don't worry, neighbor," he said to Mrs. Solymosi. "I am positive your daughter will be found. The same thing happened in Hajdunanas not long ago. A child was lost there. The whole town turned out to look for her. People said Jews got hold of her."

Mrs. Solymosi's shoulders stiffened and she stared at Mr. Scharf rigidly. He seemed oblivious of her discomfort.

"And you know what happened next?" he continued. "The girl returned home! She had fallen asleep among the weeds on the riverbank. I'm sure the same thing will happen to your daughter. She'll come home!"

He finally noticed Mrs. Solymosi's silence. A deep flush traveled up his neck and into his cheeks.

"Don't misunderstand me, missus," he stammered. "I only told you the story because I wanted to help."

When Mrs. Solymosi remained mute, he touched the brim of his hat and turned on his heels.

"Come along, Morris," he said. "I want to hear Solomon Schwarcz leading the service."

Solomon Schwarcz must be the new butcher, I thought. Morris followed his father wordlessly while Sam, still in his father's arms, stuck out his tongue.

Mrs. Csordas bustled up to us. "What did the Jew want?"

"He told us about the lost girl in Hajdunanas."

Mrs. Csordas leaned closer. "Don't you believe a word that Jew says!" Little drops of spittle sprayed from her mouth. "They're liars, every single one of them! They must have stolen that girl in Hajdunanas." She lowered her voice so I could barely hear her. "You know what these Jews do? Every year, before their Easter, they kill a Christian child and

35

use his blood to make their matzo!" She spat on the ground.

Mrs. Solymosi's face turned ashen. I caught her as she began to crumple. I sat her down, leaned her against the base of the well, and fanned her face with my apron.

"The Jews. The Jews must have killed my Esther!" she moaned. "That's why Esther didn't come home."

The women's voices rose in excitement.

Mrs. Solymosi grasped my hand and dug her nails deep into my flesh. "Did you hear that, Julie? Mrs. Csordas is right! The Jews murdered my Esther! They're the ones who killed your friend!" As she spoke her voice became stronger and full of venom. She struggled to her feet. "The Jews killed Esther for her blood!"

A murmur of assent ran through the crowd.

I realized that I knew almost nothing about the Jews among us. Except for Ma's sewing for them and me selling them eggs, I didn't have anything to do with them. I did call on Dr. Weltner when Ma got sick, but I had no choice. He was the only doctor in town. The Jews were strangers in our midst. They kept to themselves. They didn't even speak Hungarian among themselves, only German and their funny-sounding Jew language. They dressed differently from us and always kept their heads covered. Could it be possible they used our blood to make their Easter bread? If they didn't kill Esther, then who did? If she was alive, my friend would have come home. The Jews had to be responsible. There was nobody else. The Jews must have killed her.

Then I remembered how Mr. Rosenberg hired my pa to work on his farm when nobody else would give him a job and how my pa hated him for it. I remembered how Dr. Weltner gave Ma medicine without her being able to pay for it. I remembered Mrs. Scharf sending soup to Ma. Finally, I remembered the kindness in Mr. Scharf's eyes when he told us the story of the missing girl who had been found. I even thought of Morris. He had been a sweet-natured little boy. Could such people be capable of such a terrible thing? Could everybody be wrong? I didn't know what to think.

"Make no mistake about it, Mrs. Solymosi," said Mrs. Csordas. "The Jews murdered your daughter."

"How can you be so sure, Mrs. Csordas?" I asked. "I'm not saying the Jews didn't kill Esther, maybe they did, but we don't know for sure. I'm praying to the Good Lord that Esther is still alive and will come home. Mr. Scharf seems to be a kind man. I think he just wanted to set Mrs. Solymosi's mind at ease."

Mrs. Csordas jabbed me in the arm with an angry finger.

"You don't know what you're talking about. That poor child is dead. The Jews are never up to any good. I live eight steps from the synagogue and yesterday afternoon I heard faint shouts in a child's voice coming from there!" She looked around to make sure she had everybody's attention. "The voice I heard came from underground! That's not all," she continued, "I can hear their infernal praying from my house. Their service is usually finished by eleven o'clock in the morning, but yesterday they didn't leave until noon. Something must have been going on there!"

"You see, Mrs. Csordas knows the Jews are guilty!" cried Mrs. Solymosi.

She flapped her aprons in agitation.

Old Mrs. Csordas stepped closer to Esther's mother. "The Jews *must* be responsible for the disappearance of your daughter!" she said. She wagged her finger at Mrs. Solymosi. "I am warning you! You must report the Jews to the town magistrate!"

Ma was flushed and breathing heavily when I returned home. I wiped her face and hands with a damp cloth and fluffed up the pillows behind her head.

"Ma, you won't believe what happened at the well. Mrs. Csordas and Mrs. Solymosi say the Jews killed Esther."

"That's nonsense!" Ma said. "Mrs. Csordas is a foolish old busybody and you mustn't listen to her. Poor Mrs. Solymosi. She's lost her common sense because of her grief. You mustn't pay attention to her either."

"But, Ma, everybody says the Jews killed Esther!"

She raised herself to her elbows with great effort.

"People can be foolish. They don't know much about the Jews, although they've lived among us for as long as I can remember. Tisza-Eszlar is as much their home as ours. They are ordinary people, both good and bad. They aren't devils who would do the terrible thing they are accused of."

She smiled. "Wasn't Mrs. Scharf kind to send me soup? Morris was a good boy. Do you remember playing with him in Mrs. Rosenberg's garden?"

"I just saw him, Ma, with his father."

I told her what Mr. Scharf had said to Esther's mother.

"I've never met Mr. Scharf, but I hear he is a good man. It sounds to me as if he was just trying to put Mrs. Solymosi's mind to rest."

Her voice faltered and she licked her chapped lips.

I filled a cup with water, but she waved it away.

"It's foolish to blame the Jews," she said and closed her eyes.

I hurried to get Clara ready for church.

CHAPTER 5

THURSDAY, APRIL 27, 1882

Ma tossed and turned in her sleep all night, waking me repeatedly. I was grateful that Pa and Clara slept through her restlessness.

The next morning, after Pa had left for work, I helped Clara get dressed and gave her breakfast. I went to rouse Ma. I kissed her on her cheek and waited for her eyes to fly open.

"It's time to get up, Ma!"

She gave a sleepy moan. I shook her arm, but she didn't respond. "Ma, Ma! Wake up!" I remembered that when Clara was a baby, Ma would wake her up in order to nurse her by applying cold, wet rags to the bottoms of her feet. I dampened my apron and held it to Ma's feet, but she only groaned.

I stood by her bed wringing my hands. If I went to get Pa, he'd beat me for sure for bothering him at work. It was clear I had to do something. Ma was moaning and wouldn't wake up. I would have to fetch Dr. Weltner. He had helped Ma before, and I prayed to the Good Lord he would help her again. I scooped Clara up into my arms and ran to the doctor's house.

"Where are you taking me?" she asked as I pulled her closer to me.

"Ma doesn't feel good. I'm going to fetch Dr. Weltner. He'll know what to do."

"Pa'll be mad!" Clara said, a scared look on her face.

"I don't care! I just want Ma to be better. You mustn't tell Pa."

"I won't!" she promised and hugged my neck so tightly I could barely breathe.

I loosened her fingers.

"Don't worry! Everything will be fine!"

My words didn't sound convincing even in my own ears. Although she was very thin, Clara was still heavy to carry, but I didn't put her down. The beating of her heart against mine made me feel a little less frightened.

Dr. Weltner's handsome house was near the synagogue. I rapped on the front door. An old woman opened it a crack and stuck her head out.

"What can I do for you?" she asked.

I had to catch my breath before speaking.

"Would you like a drink of water? Is the child sick?" She held out her arms to Clara.

I put Clara down. She burrowed her face in my skirt.

"No, missus. It's my ma! I can't wake her up!"

"The doctor is out now, but fortunately for you, he is close by." She pointed to the shabby house next to the synagogue. "Mrs. Scharf is having her baby." She shook her head sadly. "He's been over there for a long time," she added. "You're welcome to wait for him inside."

I looked at my bare feet. They were dusty. My skirt and blouse were covered in patches. Clara was in an old dress and her pinafore was stained from her breakfast.

"Thank you, missus, but we'll wait outside. We don't want to mess up your clean floors."

"Nonsense! Come on in."

She flung the door wide open.

"We'll stay outside. I am scared that we might miss the doctor when he is done at Mrs. Scharf's. He might go somewhere else without telling you."

She chuckled. "I can see that you're a sharp young woman," she said. "It's not likely that he would go anywhere else without letting me know, but suit yourself. Knock on the door if you change your mind about coming in."

Clara and I settled down on the steps in front of the house. Jewish men in long black coats were hurrying into the synagogue. Across the street, old Mrs. Goldberg, in a shapeless dress, her head covered by a scarf, was sweeping her front steps. She was one of my egg customers. She always made a big fuss if they weren't large enough and argued about their price. When I called hello, she sniffed but did not reply.

A boy was playing with marbles in front of the Scharfs' house. It was Sam.

"Hey, Sam, what are you doing?"

He looked up but didn't answer. I tried again.

"Can we play marbles with you?"

"My mama says not to play with strangers," he mumbled.

"We're not strangers! Don't you remember that we spoke to your pa at the well?"

He thought for a moment, then held out a marble to me.

I kneeled down and began to play with him. Clara sat on the ground beside us, watching wide-eyed, her thumb in her mouth. We must have been at our game for close to a half-hour when a tap on my shoulder made me jump and the marble I was shooting rolled in the wrong direction.

"Why are you playing with the Jew boy?" It was Elizabeth Sos. Her mother was another of my customers. Elizabeth looked me over from head to toe. Even though she was two years younger than me, she always made me aware of my rumpled clothes and dirty feet. I stole a jealous glance at her frilly white dress and shiny black boots. She was accompanied by Miss Farkas, the village magistrate's sister, and two other women I did not recognize.

"What's your name, girl?" Miss Farkas barked.

"I am Julie Vamosi, missus, and this is my sister, Clara."

Elizabeth gave Miss Farkas a meaningful glance.

"Should we?" she asked, nodding her head toward Sam.

"Of course," Miss Farkas said. "These girls are peasants, of no importance at all!"

She turned her back on me and patted Sam on the head.

"Hello, Sam," she said, her voice syrupy. "What are you doing?"

I wondered how she knew his name. Sam was mute, his head hanging. Finely dressed ladies did not chat with little Jewish boys.

"Don't be scared of us," said Elizabeth. "We're your friends."

She crouched down beside us, gingerly lifting her skirt out of the dust.

"I'll play with you," she said.

She picked up one of the marbles from the dirt carefully.

"What should I do with this marble?" she asked.

"Why does the girl want to play with us?" Sam asked.

Clara reached out and touched Elizabeth's sleeve.

"You're pretty," she said.

Elizabeth pushed her hand away.

"Don't touch me with your filthy hands! You'll get me dirty!"

Clara began to cry.

"Silence!" Miss Farkas thundered.

Elizabeth was rubbing her sleeve sulkily but did not answer back.

Miss Farkas reached into her reticule, pulled out a package of sweets, and gave Sam a candy. She then offered the sweets to her friends, but not to Clara or me. Clara opened her mouth to ask for a piece, but I clamped my hand over her lips before she could say anything.

Sam held the candy in his palm and stared at it.

Miss Farkas laughed. "Why, the little savage doesn't know what to do with the candy!"

Her companions tittered.

"You have to suck on the sweet, little boy." Sam finally popped it into his mouth. His eyes grew round with delight as the sugar dissolved on his tongue.

"The candy is good, isn't it?" she asked.

Sam nodded.

"How old are you?" Miss Farkas asked.

Sam didn't reply.

"How old are you?" she repeated more sharply.

"Tell her your age!" I whispered in his ear.

"I be five," mumbled Sam.

"I want to talk to you, Sam," Miss Farkas said. "I want to tell you a secret!"

Sam looked confused, on the verge of tears.

"Sam, do you know a servant girl by the name of Esther Solymosi?" Miss Farkas asked.

Sam shook his head.

"Esther's mother came to see my brother, the village magistrate," Miss Farkas said in a self-important voice. I could see her chest puff out. "Mrs. Solymosi told my brother that her daughter disappeared. Nobody knows where she is!"

Sam just stared at her, bewildered.

Miss Farkas smiled. Her expression made me think of a cat toying with a mouse.

"Would you like to have another sweetie, Sam?"

45

She pushed another candy into his hand. He ate it greedily.

"I want to tell you a secret," she said. "Do you want to know my secret? If you listen carefully to it, I'll give you more sweets."

Sam nodded eagerly.

"A little bird told me that your papa called Esther Solymosi into the synagogue," she said, pointing at the building next door. "Once she was inside, he tied her up with a rope and the new Jew butcher cut her!"

Sam began to cry. Miss Farkas pressed another sweet into his palm.

Elizabeth spoke up. "The same birdie told me that your papa forced Esther into a chair and held her head while your big brother, Morris, held down her hands. Then your butcher cut her leg," she said breathlessly. "When they finished with her, all three of them carried her toward a tall tree!"

"I want Mama!" Sam said and cried even harder. "I want my mama!"

"Why are you saying such terrible things to him?" I pulled Sam to me. "He is just a little boy! Why are you trying to scare him?"

"Silence, you stupid girl!" said Miss Farkas.

Before I could reply, the front door to the Scharfs' house swung open and a grim-faced Dr. Weltner appeared on the threshold. Mr. Scharf, his eyes red-rimmed, was beside him.

"Come into the house immediately, Sam!" he said sternly.

Sam gave a scared look in Miss Farkas's direction, gathered up his marbles, and ran into the house, followed by his father. The door clicked close behind them.

Dr. Weltner tipped his hat at Miss Farkas and her companions and set out for his home. I ran after him, dragging Clara behind me. I tugged on his sleeve. He stopped.

"What can I do for you?" he asked courteously. "You're Mrs. Vamosi's girl, aren't you?" he said, taking a closer look at me.

I told him that we'd been waiting for him because I couldn't wake up Ma.

"I'm surprised that this didn't happen much sooner." He sighed. "What a horrible day! First, Mr. Scharf's poor baby boy, and now this." He wiped his face with his handkerchief. "Wait here. I'll get my buggy and we'll be on our way."

We were home in a few minutes, but it didn't make a difference. We were too late. Our ma had gone to the angels.

CHAPTER 6

MONDAY, MAY 8, 1882

Pa was walking, his hat in his hand, behind the horse-drawn cart that carried Ma's casket. Next to him was his sister, our stern-faced Aunt Irma. Clara and I followed them. Clara clung to my hand, her face grimy from her weeping. I was glad of the clop-clopping of the horse's hooves as it masked my sobs.

Several villagers joined the procession as we made our way to the Roman Catholic cemetery at the edge of town. Pa turned his head to look behind us, his face blank. When I had gone to fetch him at Mr. Rosenberg's farm, his face was expressionless as I told him Ma had gone to heaven. If I hadn't noticed the tremor that ran through his body, I would've thought he hadn't even heard me. He'd had the same blank look ever since.

Father Gabor was waiting for us beside the open grave. As he began to pray, I looked around. I was surprised by the number of people who had come to pay their last respects to my ma. Across from us, Sophie Solymosi was standing beside her mother and her brother, Janos. She smiled at me sadly. Five terrible weeks had passed since Esther had disappeared. She must have been wondering whether it would be her family's turn at a funeral next. I saw Dr. Weltner at the back of the crowd. He lifted his arm in my direction when our eyes met.

I pulled Clara closer to my side as the casket was lowered into the ground. As shovelfuls of dirt landed on top of it with loud thuds, I remembered the thudding noise the bread dough used to make when Ma kneaded it before it became a delicious loaf of dark bread under her skillful hands.

As the earth rained down on the casket, I remembered how thunder and lightning used to scare me when I was still a little girl and how Ma would swoop me into the safety of her arms and tell me stories about her childhood until I would forget the drum-drumming of the rain on the thatched roof.

As the priest's voice droned on in prayer, I remembered the times when Ma would hold my hands as we danced around the yard, scattering the chickens, singing silly songs out of the sheer joy of being alive.

The casket was finally covered by mounds of earth. I hoped that Ma's spirit would not mind the weight of the dirt on top of it. My ma never liked to be weighed down.

She even complained if she had to drape her heavy wool shawl over her slight shoulders in the winter.

We walked back to our house. Neighbors had brought us food for the funeral meal. There was goose liver from Mrs. Pasztar who lived down the street. Mrs. Solymosi had baked two loaves of bread. I was sure that she would go hungry because of it. Even Mrs. Huri brought along a pitcher of milk. The room buzzed with subdued conversation and a few bursts of quickly suppressed laughter. I was occupied with spreading the pork fat that Farmer Veres had brought on slices of black bread to hand around. I was glad that my hands were busy because they kept me from thinking about the funeral. That would come later.

"Do you need help?" asked Sophie.

I handed her the pitcher of milk and she poured it into tin cups. When we finished, we arranged the bread and the cups of milk on tin plates and we walked around the room offering the victuals to the mourners. Clara followed me, clutching at my skirt. She would not let go. After a while, I forgot she was there.

I could hear Mrs. Solymosi's voice.

"I have witnesses!" Mrs. Solymosi had said the words so often they sounded like a dreadful song. "The Jews hurt Esther. The Jews are responsible. They must pay for what they did to her!"

Her hands were balled into fists and her voice rose in a loud crescendo. All eyes were fixed on her.

I tapped her on the shoulder and held out my plate.

"Something to eat, ladies," I suggested.

Greedy hands reached for the food, but Mrs. Solymosi was unstoppable.

"The Jews took away Esther. They consumed my daughter. They must be punished! I went to Vencsello and spoke to the district magistrate. He promised me that he will investigate the Jews.

"The little Scharf boy, Sam, told Miss Farkas and Elizabeth Sos what the Jews did. He told Miss Farkas they lured my Esther into their temple and then his father and his brother held her down while their butcher cut her!" Her voice broke and she began to weep. "The Jews must be punished for killing my darling girl! They killed her for her virgin blood, to use it in their Easter bread!"

Her companions, who had heard this many times before, were nodding in a sympathetic chorus. I weighed my words carefully before speaking.

"I'm not saying the Jews didn't murder Esther, but that's not what Sam said. Clara and I were there when Miss Farkas and Elizabeth talked to him. They put words –"

A heavy hand squeezed my shoulder hard. It was Pa.

"Shut your mouth, you foolish girl!" he grunted.

I fell silent.

"The girl is young, please excuse her," said Aunt Irma. "She doesn't know what she's saying."

Clara burrowed her face in my skirt.

"Sam Scharf told me the same thing he told you, Mrs. Solymosi," said Mrs. Pasztar. "I was driving my geese past

51

the Scharfs' house a few days ago when Sam ran into the street and scattered my geese. He must have been waiting for me in the window, the young hellion!"

"He is only five."

A look from Pa stopped me.

Mrs. Pasztar's eyes traveled around the room. When she was certain she had everyone's attention, she began again.

"I was so angry! I knew how difficult it would be to find all my geese. I swished my stick at the boy. I only wished that I could have made it meet his behind, but he ran away from me, yelling, 'Just for that, I won't tell you what my father did to that servant girl.'"

Stunned silence greeted her words until Mrs. Huri spoke.

"Poor, dear Esther," she said. "The Jews must be responsible for her disappearance!"

"There is no question about that!" said a farmer.

How could they be so sure? I asked myself. I opened my mouth but thought better of it. I rubbed my shoulder gently. It was still tender.

The next hour seemed to last forever, but finally the last of the guests was gone. The cottage echoed of silence. It was as if Ma had never been with us, except in my heart.

I barely slept that night, my mind a jumble of grief and fear. I thought of my ma and how I would never see her again. I felt so alone. What would happen to Clara and me without her love and guidance? I didn't even have Esther to turn to. I wondered if Pa and our neighbors were right when they accused the Jews of murdering my dear friend.

Ma believed in the Jews' innocence. I didn't know what to believe myself.

The next morning, Aunt Irma's husband arrived in a donkey cart to take Clara to their home in Csonkafuzes.

"Pack up your sister's things," Pa said to me. "Clara will be living with your Aunt Irma from now on."

"What do you mean?"

"Are you deaf, girl?" Spittle flew from his mouth. "You'll do as you're told!"

Clara sensed that something was terribly wrong and screamed as loudly as she could.

She had to be carried kicking and crying into the donkey cart. I stood in the street waving until the buggy became a small dot in the landscape. My promises to visit wafted after her in the air.

Pa was waiting for me in the house.

"Now, pack up your own belongings," he said. "Starting tomorrow, you'll be working at the town jail. Sergeant Toth's housekeeper is away. You'll be taking her place."

—

CHAPTER 7

SATURDAY, MAY 20, 1882

The jail was empty except for old Mr. Meszaros, who got drunk every Friday, slept in the jail overnight, and was taken home by his long-suffering wife on Saturday morning.

Life in the prison was much easier than life with Pa had been. As long as I swept up the cells and cooked his meals, Sergeant Toth left me alone. Nobody hit me. There was no one to fear.

Toth was a quiet man. Whole days would pass without the two of us exchanging a single word. He communicated with grunts and nods. A grunt and a glance at the floor meant that I had sweeping to do. Another grunt and a rubbing of his stomach signaled it was time for his dinner of potatoes and sausage. Anything left over, I was allowed to have. After a few days, I found myself having long, loud conversations with Ma and Clara. My only thoughts were of my sister and how frightened she must be. I tried to think of a way to visit her at Csonkafuzes, but Toth did not pay me a salary and I was given no time off from my job. She might as well have been sent across the sea.

I rarely left the jail because the sergeant let me use one of the empty cells as my living quarters. He even gave me a straw-filled burlap bag to sleep on. I set up two wooden crates to serve as a table and chair and tied my spare vest to the steel bars over the window to keep out curious stares. I folded Ma's shawl carefully and draped it over her workbox. The shawl and the workbox were precious to me. They were the only belongings of Ma's I had.

On a beautiful, sunny May morning, Sergeant Toth shocked me by talking to me directly. I had just put his breakfast in front of him when he caught a corner of my apron.

"Go to Kohlmayer's," he grunted, "and bring me back rope. Kohlmayer will know how much to give you," he added, handing me a coin.

I was so startled by hearing a full sentence from him I didn't move for a moment. He waved his knife and fork at me.

"Go!" he said. "Go!"

I didn't need a second prompting.

I had hardly left the jail since I started to work for Sergeant Toth so I dawdled as much as I dared in the sunshine. I skipped along the dusty street, skirting a gaggle of geese before knocking on the Rosenbergs' door. Sophie answered. She was neatly dressed in a black skirt and white blouse. Rosie Rosenberg was right behind her.

"Julie! Come in, come in," Sophie said.

"My mama baked an apple strudel and we were just going to eat a slice. Come and share it with us," said Rosie.

My mouth watered at her words, and before long we were sitting around the kitchen table with generous helpings of the flaky strudel in front of us.

I leaned back and sighed contentedly.

"I must go," I said with regret. "Sergeant Toth will be impatient if I don't get back from my errand."

"He won't even notice you're gone," laughed Rosie. "His noggin is always in the clouds. I don't understand how he prevents the prisoners from escaping!"

"What prisoners? The jail is always empty except for old Meszaros."

"Where are you heading?" Sophie asked.

"To Kohlmayer's. The warden asked me to buy rope."

Sophie looked stricken. Esther's last trip had also been to Kohlmayer's.

She stood up from the table and walked over to the window, her back to us. When she finally turned around, her eyes were bright with unshed tears.

"They're still looking for Esther, but they'll never find her," she said. "If Esther were alive she would have come home."

"What do you mean? Who is searching for her?"

"The district court in Nyiregyhaza sent two men to Tisza-Eszlar to look into Esther's disappearance. They're going all over town asking questions about her," said Rosie. "They came here yesterday. Sophie and I told them we met Esther on her way home from Kohlmayer's. She didn't stop long to talk to us because she didn't want to keep Mrs. Huri waiting."

"I'll never forget how miserable she looked," said Sophie. She dabbed her eyes. "She wouldn't tell us what was bothering her. I should have kept asking till she did!"

The kitchen door opened and Mrs. Rosenberg came into the room.

"Miss Kelemen has arrived, Rosie. She is waiting for you," she said.

Rosie grimaced. "Please send her away, Mama. You know how much I hate the piano!"

"All well-brought-up young ladies play the piano," said Mrs. Rosenberg in a tone that brooked no arguments.

Rosie followed her mother out of the room sullenly. I stood up.

"I have to go too."

Sophie grabbed my hand and leaned so close her lips were almost touching my face.

"They killed Esther," she whispered. "They killed my sister for her blood. They wanted her blood to make their Easter bread."

I stared at her flushed cheeks, the feverish glint in her eyes.

"They? Who are they? What are you talking about?"

"The Jews of course. They killed my sister."

"You don't know that for sure. My ma said the Jews shouldn't be blamed. I don't know what to think, but I do know that Rosie is a Jew and she didn't kill your sister. I'd bet my last forint, if I had one, that neither did her mother or father. They treat you like a daughter."

"The Rosenbergs might not be responsible, but everybody knows the Jews killed my sister. I overheard my master tell my mistress that even some of the newspapers in Budapest are accusing the Jews of killing Esther for her blood," she said stubbornly. "I went with Rosie to their Jew church once. They do strange things there. And they speak in gibberish. You can't understand a single word they're saying."

"But that doesn't mean –" I stopped mid-sentence. I could see by the firmness of her expression that it was useless trying to continue the discussion, so I said a hasty good-bye and left.

The way to Kohlmayer's passed by the synagogue. As I approached, I saw a commotion around the building. The synagogue was surrounded by uniformed gendarmes equipped with spades and shovels. They were digging up the small garden between the synagogue wall and Mrs. Csordas's house no farther than eight steps away.

I crossed the road to get a closer look. The door of the synagogue was open. Inside, a tall man dressed in city clothes was running his fingers along the walls. When he turned toward his companion, I saw his face. He was a youngish man with a neatly combed mustache and beard. His eyes bulged behind rimless spectacles, making him look like an evil toad.

"Nothing! There is nothing here!" He slapped his thigh in frustration. "We dredged the Tisza and found nothing. We dug up all new graves in the Jewish cemetery and found nothing!"

"We are missing something, Bary," said the other man. "The girl couldn't have disappeared into thin air. The Jews must have repainted the wall where her blood spattered. There should be an indentation on the floor where they buried her."

"You would think so, wouldn't you, Peczely?" Bary said. "These cursed people are too cunning to leave any evidence behind!"

"What about those shovel marks outside?"

"The gendarmes aren't finding anything there either," Bary said. "I'll have them dig up the courtyard next. If it takes me till eternity, I'll find the body of that poor girl – even if I have to have the Tisza dredged again. These murderers won't get the best of me!"

Bary's eyes burned in his face with such fanatic zeal that I stepped back to increase the distance between us. My elbow caught a shovel leaning against the synagogue door and it clattered loudly to the ground. The men turned toward me.

"Who are you?" said Bary. "What are you doing here? Be gone!"

I broke into a run and didn't stop till, breathless, I reached Kohlmayer's. I waited for my turn in an agony of impatience – Kohlmayer liked to chat with his customers.

The shadows were lengthening by the time I got back to the jail, which was no longer empty. The gendarmes had arrested Joseph Scharf, his wife, and Morris and Sam. They had also arrested Solomon Schwarcz, the new butcher. They had even arrested Abraham Buxbaum and Lipot Braun, the men who had applied unsuccessfully for the Jew butcher's job.

—

CHAPTER 8

SATURDAY, MAY 20, 1882 – SUNDAY, MAY 21, 1882

I stood on the threshold of the kitchen of the Tisza-Eszlar jail and stared at the chaos around me. The room was filled with gendarmes in uniforms and the Jewish prisoners. The lamentations of the Jews were loud, but the jailors' curses were louder still.

"We're innocent! We've done nothing! Let us go!" Joseph Scharf's face was so distorted by anguish I barely recognized him.

Each of the men had long forelocks and were dressed in their Sabbath best with black hats atop their heads.

"It is the Sabbath! You must release us! We belong in the synagogue today," said a small man with a long black beard.

"Sei ruhig, Solomon!" said one of the men. "Can't you see that it's useless to plead with them? You're just making them angrier!"

Mrs. Scharf was cowering in a corner beside the stove. Her handsome head was covered by a dark kerchief. Her arms were wrapped around a weeping Sam. Morris stood beside her, his face pale. He was trembling.

"Stop that caterwauling!" cried the frog-eyed man I had seen at the synagogue. The prisoners fell silent. The only sounds were little Sam's sobs.

"Why is everybody in the kitchen?" I asked one of the gendarmes.

"It's the largest room in the prison. We needed the space for all these people."

The man with the frog's eyes must have heard us.

"Who are you?" he asked. "I've seen you before . . ."

"She is my servant, Mr. Bary," said Sergeant Toth. He turned to me. "We're hungry, girl! Prepare us some food."

I hurried to the stove, thanking the Blessed Virgin under my breath that I had remembered to peel a bucket of potatoes while I was preparing the sergeant's breakfast. There was also a slab of bacon I had not yet cooked. I would fry it up with the potatoes for the gentlemen from the city.

While I was slicing the potatoes, Sam's sobs gave way to the panicky hysteria of a terrified small child. I shot him an encouraging smile, but he ignored me. Morris was biting his fingers.

"Clear the room! Take the Jews to the cells!" Bary commanded. "I want to talk to the two boys alone!"

Mrs. Scharf pulled her young son even closer.

"Please, sir, I beg you. Please let my little boy stay with me!"

"The children's place is with us," said her husband. "Leave my children alone!"

A gendarme tore Sam out of Mrs. Scharf's arms, and within minutes all of the Jews except the boys were shoved and kicked out of the kitchen.

The potatoes were hissing on the fire so loudly I had to strain to hear.

Bary took Sam by the hand and placed him on his knee. Sam hiccuped and tried to catch his breath.

"Now, Sam, tell me exactly what you told Miss Farkas," Bary said. "Tell me about your father and Esther Solymosi, the servant girl who disappeared."

I saw Morris step toward Mr. Bary with clenched fists. I caught hold of his arm and yanked it hard. I put my finger to my lips before he could open his mouth. Fortunately, Bary's attention was focused on Sam. Morris's face was flushed and he was breathing hard, but he lowered his hands and remained silent.

"Now listen to me, boy!" Bary said to Sam in an angry voice. "Did you tell Miss Farkas that your pa called Esther Solymosi into the synagogue where he tied her up with a rope? And did you tell her that your pa held her head

63

and your brother, Morris, held her hands while Solomon Schwarcz cut her leg? Did you also say they drained her blood into a pot? And after they finished with her they carried her toward a tall tree?"

I wanted to shout that I had heard Miss Farkas and Elizabeth Sos tell Sam that the butcher Schwarcz had cut Esther's leg. It wasn't Sam who had said it. All he had done was cry. However, after a quick glance at Bary's fierce face, I kept quiet. I bent over the sizzling potatoes once again.

Sam didn't answer Bary. He closed his eyes, his cries fading to whimpers. Bary's fingers tightened on the boy's leg.

"Did you tell all of that to Miss Farkas?" he asked.

"Yes," Sam whispered .

"Yes what?" Bary roared. "Your brother held Esther's hands, didn't he?"

"Yes," replied Sam.

"No, Sam, no! No say lies!" cried Morris. "Was machst du?"

Bary pointed his finger at Morris. "Shut him up! Sergeant Toth, silence him!"

The sergeant clasped his hand over Morris's mouth and held his arm over the boy's throat in an iron grip. Morris struggled, but he was no match for the burly officer. The meanness of Toth's expression reminded me of Pa at his angriest.

"See what can happen to you if you're not a good boy?" Bary said to Sam.

A wet stain spread over the front of the little boy's britches. Bary pushed him off his lap roughly and jumped up.

"The boy pissed himself!" he cried, rubbing at a wet spot on his trouser leg.

His companion began to laugh. He stopped himself at Bary's dark glare.

Bary crouched down and pushed his face close to Sam's.

"Listen to me, boy, and listen hard. After your father called the girl into the synagogue and tied her up, your brother held her hands and your father her head while Solomon Schwarcz killed her!" he growled. "Is that true?"

Sam's eyes were closed. If I didn't know better, I would have thought he had fallen asleep. At the same time, muffled, strangled sounds came from Morris's corner, but the sergeant was much too strong for him.

"Talk to me, boy. You better tell me what happened," yelled Bary.

"I don't know!" Sam cried.

"Your father and brother held the girl and Solomon Schwarcz killed her," Bary said, grabbing the front of Sam's shirt.

"Yes," Sam moaned.

Bary let go of Sam's shirt and as the little boy fell back Bary straightened up and spat in his face. Sam stared at him in bewilderment as his hand crept up to his wet cheek.

"Take this vermin out of my sight!" Bary ordered.

One of the gendarmes carried the child out of the room.

"I knew he'd confess!" Bary gloated.

"You're wasting your time," his companion said. "Who will believe the ranting of a five-year-old? We need an older witness!"

"You have a point, Peczely," Bary replied. He stomped back and forth the length of the room, deep in thought. "Luckily, we *do* have an older witness," he finally said. He waved his hand at Morris, still in the sergeant's grasp.

"But the boy is accused of . . ."

Bary waved his hand dismissively. "That's of no importance. Morris Scharf will be our witness. We don't need this pup. But first, let's eat. I'm hungry. Sergeant Bako!" he called to the gendarme at the door. "Fetch us some ale from the tavern we passed on our way here! Beer fit for our fine repast." He rubbed his hands.

The sudden change in his manner made me remember the food before it burnt. I began to spoon it into serving bowls.

Sergeant Toth and Peczely tied Morris's hands and feet to a chair and stuffed a rag in his mouth. Before long, all of the men were sitting down at the wooden table in the center of the room, as if they had forgotten their captive.

"I needed that!" Bary rubbed his stomach.

He took a long swig from his tankard, set it down carefully, and wiped his mustache.

"Clear the table, girl," said Sergeant Toth.

I gathered up the dirty dishes while the sergeant, almost as an afterthought, undid the ropes that tied Morris to his chair. Bary pulled the rag out of his mouth.

"So, boy," said Bary, "have you learned your lesson?"

Morris remained mute, his eyes fixed on the floor. He was trembling like a frightened animal.

"Do you admit that on the first day of April your father lured the Christian girl, Esther Solymosi, into the synagogue, where he held her head and you held her arms while the butcher Solomon Schwarcz cut her and collected her blood?"

Morris lifted up his head. His cheeks were flushed. He clasped his hands in front of his chest to steady them.

"Nein! Not true!" he said. "We did nothing! We not know girl who disappear!"

Bary ignored his reply and repeated his questions over and over again. Morris's answers didn't vary, but the life seemed to be draining from him.

Bary pulled a large watch out of his vest pocket.

"It's getting late," he said. "We'll continue with this tomorrow. A night in solitary will refresh the boy's memory!" He chuckled mirthlessly. "He'll talk tomorrow. I invited Chief Recsky to join us."

My heart filled with horror at his mention of the chief of the gendarmes. Chief Recsky was known far and wide for his cruelty.

I tossed and turned on my straw mattress that night. Morris's tormented face appeared every time I closed my eyes. When the church bells struck midnight, I got up and tiptoed to the kitchen. I was afraid to light a candle so I had to feel my way. I took the loaf of bread I was saving for Sergeant Toth's breakfast out of the cupboard and filled a small tankard with water. I was careful not to spill it as I made my way to Morris's cell.

It was so dark I could barely see Morris lying on a cot in a corner.

"Get up. Don't make any noise. I brought you some food," I whispered through the bars.

Morris sat up.

"Why you come? What you want?"

"I want to talk to you. I want to know the truth."

I passed the tankard to him. He drank greedily before passing it back to me.

"Oh, I was thirsty!" he said.

I gave him the bread. He fell on it like a hungry animal. When he finished, he wiped the back of his mouth with his hand.

"Danke. Thank you. Why you give me food?"

"I don't know. Maybe because my ma would have done the same. You and I used to play together when we were little. I want to know the truth. Tell me, what happened to Esther?"

"I not know! I not know girl. Mein Papa not know girl.

No Juden know girl. I don't understand why they say we do terrible thing."

He grabbed the bars tightly. I had to force myself not to flinch.

"They won't let me see mein Papa. Can you find out if he is treated good? Tell him Ich liebe ihn. I mean, my heart is full of feelings for him."

"You mean to say that you love your papa?"

"Yes, I want to say that. Please tell him."

I was about to say no, but then I wondered what Ma would have wanted me to do.

"I'll tell your pa," I told him.

I knew I should get back to my cell before I was discovered.

The next night it was eerily quiet as I made my way to the section of the jail where the Jewish prisoners were being held. I had just turned the corner to the hallway leading to their cells when suddenly I felt a sharp object sticking into the middle of my back.

"Halt! Where do you think you are going?"

I froze. What should I say? I yawned and rubbed my eyes.

"Who are you? What are you doing in my bedroom?" I kept rubbing my eyes.

"Turn around!"

I found myself staring into a guard's rifle barrel.

"What do you mean why am I in your bedroom? Are you daft, girl?"

I looked around me, trying to appear confused.

"Where am I?"

"In the corridor leading to the Jews' cells," the guard answered roughly.

I forced myself to cry. It wasn't hard – all I had to do was think of what would happen to me if Sergeant Toth found out I'd been stealing food to give to Morris and was about to carry a message to his father.

"Dear Mother of God," I said, "I must have walked in my sleep again!" It wasn't hard for me to sound flustered and frightened.

"Get back to your room or you'll regret it!" the guard hollered.

Morris would be disappointed that I couldn't pass on his message, but I had to follow the guard's orders.

CHAPTER 9

SUNDAY, MAY 21, 1882

I had just returned from church and was tying on my apron when I heard Sergeant Toth calling me.

"Water, girl! Bring us a bucket of water!"

I hurried to his office, the cold water splashing over my bare toes. Gendarme Bako was guarding the door. When he let me in, I put down the pail heavily to prevent it from spilling even more. Morris was lying on the floor, senseless, Chief Recsky looming over him. Bary and Peczely were circling around them, like tigers in a cage. Toth was leaning back on a wooden chair in the corner.

Morris was lying on his side, his knees to his chest and his arms over his face. Chief Recsky grabbed the pail and swung the water at him. Morris coughed and spluttered.

Recsky picked up a whip lying on the table and flicked it in the direction of Morris's head. Morris tried to protect his eyes. Recsky laughed harshly. An expression of distaste flitted over Bary's face, but Peczely was expressionless.

"Talk, boy!" Recsky said. "Tell us how you held down the servant girl while the others butchered her!"

Morris struggled into a sitting position.

"We not do that!" he said. His voice was steady, but he was trembling. "I tell you, we never see girl! We not know her – not me, not Papa, not Solomon Schwarcz!"

"Liar!" Recsky said, leaning closer to the boy. "Tell the truth or I'll have you taken to the district prison in Nyiregyhaza. I'll have you locked up there till the end of your days." His voice rose. "Tell the truth or I'll throw away the keys to your cell!"

Suddenly, almost nonchalantly, he kicked him in the stomach. Morris doubled up, moaning.

"Will you talk now?"

"I'm sorry, but I tell truth," Morris gasped.

"Stop it!" Bary said. "Can't you see that the boy won't confess? I don't care for such brutality!"

"You can't be lily-livered, Bary, not if you want the whelp to tell you how they killed the girl," said Recsky. "The boy is all we have. Nothing was found in Scharf's house. I even had my men dig up his dead baby's grave. We found nothing! We dredged the Tisza again. If the body of the girl is under the water, it's nothing more than food for the fishes by now. The boy's all we got," he repeated.

Bary drew himself up.

"Remember whom you're addressing, Chief Recsky!"

The chief gendarme glared at him but fell silent.

"Take the boy back to his cell," he finally growled.

I stepped aside while Gendarme Bako pushed and shoved Morris out of the room. The boy was barely able to walk.

Recsky finally noticed my presence. "Why are you still here?" he asked. "Get out!"

I obeyed him immediately.

I dreamt of Clara again that night. She was dressed in rags and called out to me.

"Help me, Julie! I need you!" she pleaded. "Take me away from here."

She held out her arms, but as I ran to her she disappeared. I woke up sweating in spite of the chill air. The need to hold her in my arms overwhelmed me.

There was loud banging and talking in the street under my window. I pushed the wooden box that served as my table under it and climbed up on top. I pulled aside the vest that acted as a curtain and peeked through the bars. A horse-drawn cart filled with hay was parked next to the prison. Morris, his arms in chains, was being led toward it by Gendarme Bako.

"How long we go to Nyiregyhaza?" he asked the gendarme.

"Shut your mouth! It'll take as long as it takes," Bako said as he pushed Morris into the cart.

Morris lay on the straw, shielding his face from Bako's blows with his shackled hands. Recsky and Peczely came out of the prison by a side door and climbed up to the seat beside Bako. Bako pulled in the reins and the cart started to move.

"Good-bye, Morris!" I called through the bars. "Good-bye!"

"Good-bye, Julie!" said Morris. "I do no wrong!"

The crack of Recsky's whip silenced him.

I watched the cart lurch away down the rutted road. I climbed off the box and lay down on my cot, but I couldn't fall asleep again. At first I felt sorry for Morris, but then I started wondering what if he *did* lie and the Jews *did* kill Esther? Somebody did, or she would have returned home! I wished I knew what to believe.

CHAPTER 10

—

MONDAY, MAY 22, 1882

I woke up before the roosters the next morning, aching for
Clara. I had to see her. My only hope was Pa. Maybe I could
convince him to help me get to Aunt Irma's. I dressed
quickly. I knew I didn't have much time. I had to be back at
the jail to serve Sergeant Toth his breakfast, but I had to talk
to Pa first. I knew he was as likely to beat me as to help me,
but I didn't care. I was desperate to hold Clara and to know
she was all right.

I untied my vest from the bars over the window and
quickly put it on to ward off the gentle breeze of the spring
dawn. I draped Ma's shawl over my shoulders. I didn't really
need it, but I felt close to her when I wore it. For a moment,
I buried my face in its softness and engulfed myself in her
scent. It felt as if she had her arms around me.

The moon was still in the sky as I ran barefoot through the empty streets, but Pa left for the fields early. I was surprised that the windows of the house were dark. I banged on the door, but Pa didn't open it. When I tried the latch, the door swung open so I went in.

The smell of rotting food made my nostrils twitch. Despite the moonlight sneaking through the narrow windows, the room was dark. For a moment I thought I'd missed Pa and he'd already gone to work. It took a few moments for my eyes to adjust to the darkness. Pa was lying in his bed, next to the wall. His mouth was wide open and he was snoring loudly. A tankard was overturned on the floor beside the bed. I could smell the stink of the ale even across the room.

Pa wasn't alone. Next to him lay a yellow-haired woman I had never seen before. Her skirts were immodestly bundled up around her hips, leaving her legs bare. I quickly turned to leave.

The woman stirred.

"Who are you?" she asked, her words slurred with sleep.

"I'm Julie. Who are *you?*"

"Ah, the daughter!" she snickered but didn't pull her skirts down. "I'm your pa's friend."

She nudged Pa with her elbow.

"Wake up, Peter!"

Pa opened his eyes. When he saw me, he struggled to sit up.

"What're you doing here?"

The woman laughed. It made me so angry I stepped

even closer. I could smell the drink on Pa's sour breath.

"Has Sergeant Toth thrown you out? You can't come back here! You'll be sorry if Toth stops sending your wages to me!"

It took me a moment to find the right words.

"What wages, Pa?"

"Stop your infernal questions!" he roared. He swung his legs around to the side of the bed and stood up.

"If you didn't lose your job, what are you doing here? Why are you spying on me?"

"I'm not spying, Pa. I came to ask you if there's any news of Clara."

"None of your damned business! Get out of my sight!"

The woman tugged on his arm. "Is that the shawl you were telling me about?"

My hand was on the door latch when Pa grabbed my arm, his fingers digging into my flesh.

"Give that to me!" he roared, yanking the shawl off my shoulders.

"Pa, what are you doing? Give me back Ma's shawl! She wanted me to have it! Please, Pa! Give it back to me!"

He opened the door and pushed me into the dawn. I heard the key turn in the lock as I tumbled down the steps, scraping my knees.

I banged on the door with all my might.

"Please, Pa! Please! Give me back Ma's shawl!"

There was no answer. After a long time, I limped back to the jail, crying the entire way.

Sergeant Toth ate his breakfast as if he had never seen food before. Half of his meal was gone before he noticed I was still standing in front of him. He stared at me wordlessly. I took a deep breath.

"I was wondering if I could have part of my pay, sir."

"You get room and board!" He lowered his spoon. "You won't have to worry about your job much longer. My house-keeper will be coming back in a few days."

It took a moment for me to understand what he was saying. It was a calamity. I couldn't go back to Pa. He didn't want me. And as for making a home for Clara, that hope vanished like my dreams of the poor child.

"Go do your job, while you still have one!"

He picked up his spoon and attacked his meal again, as if I wasn't there. I was at the door when one of the jail guards rushed into the office.

"They brought the Jew boy back, sir! He confessed!" he said. "Mr. Bary ordered me to round up all the Jewish men in town and line them up in front of the jail."

Toth stood.

"Have you done it?"

"I wanted to check first with you, sir."

"Do as Bary says."

In less than a half-hour, every Jewish man in Tisza-Eszlar was lined up in front of the jail – the farmers, the butcher, Dr. Weltner. The Jewish prisoners had been herded out of the jail to stand with them. Gendarmes were pointing their rifles at the frightened men. The street around the jail was full of angry, menacing villagers. I saw Pa, but although he must have noticed me he turned his head away. Jewish wives and children clung to one another at the back, craning to see the men through the milling crowd. Sam and Mrs. Scharf were among them. It was only then that I realized they had been released from jail.

I could see Bary, Recsky, and Peczely, their heads together on the jail stairs, conferring. At Bary's side, Morris was bent over, clutching his stomach. He looked up, his face bruised and one of his eyes swollen shut.

Bary called to me. "Bring us some water, girl!"

I hefted the pail and cup by my feet. As I filled the cup for Bary, I whispered to Morris, "What happened to you? Why did you confess?"

"Silence! Don't answer her!" ordered Recsky.

I scuttled away with the pail.

Morris swayed and fell to his knees. Mr. Scharf broke away from the gendarmes.

"Leave my poor boy alone!"

"Papa! Papa!" wept Morris as the gendarmes caught Mr. Scharf and dragged him back to the other prisoners.

"Let my papa go!" begged Morris. "Please, let him go! I change my mind!" He turned to Recsky. "I no confess anymore!" he said.

"Changed your mind? Take back your confession? You can't do that!" roared the chief.

"You told me that the boy confessed of his own free will," said Bary, low and furious. "The confession has to be voluntary for it to stand up in a court of law."

"Don't be a fool, Bary," said Peczely. "The boy's confession is signed and sealed. You saw it with your own eyes."

Morris struggled to his feet.

"I lie! I lie when I tell you that we kill girl who missing. We never meet her!" he shouted. The villagers hooted and swore. "I lie because I want you to stop beating me! You say you not hurt my papa if I sign paper! You say you let my papa go! That's why I sign paper you give me."

Recsky lifted his whip high.

"Stop it! Stop it, Recsky!" ordered Bary.

"Let me talk to the boy," Peczely said.

He leaned close to Morris's ear. I stood so near them I could hear him speak.

"Listen, boy, if you don't stop your foolishness we will put you and your father back in jail and throw away the keys," he said. "Do you want that on your conscience?"

"No, no!" mumbled Morris. "I'm sorry!"

Peczely leaned even closer to Morris. "If you don't tell us which of these men killed Esther Solymosi, your father will feel the sting of the chief gendarme's whip even more than you have. Do you want that on your conscience?" he repeated. "Am I making myself clear?"

"Yes. I'm sorry for being so fool," Morris begged. "Forgive me!"

Peczely's smile made me shiver.

"I'm glad that you came to your senses, boy, before it was too late" he said pleasantly. "Just do what you're supposed to do and then both you and your father will be fine. Are you ready to cooperate?"

"Yes, forgive me!" Morris pleaded.

Peczely turned to Recsky and Bary.

"The boy has seen reason," he said. "Let's begin."

Bary walked up to the line of Jewish men. Recsky's hand gripped Morris's arm as he dragged him along.

Two Jewish men were holding up a weeping Joseph Scharf. They fell silent as Bary approached.

"Attention!" Bary's eyes bulged behind his rimless glasses. "You vermin claim ignorance about the disappearance of the servant girl Esther Solymosi, but I know you are lying!"

The villagers shouted their approval. "Death to the Jews! Death to the Jews!" they chanted.

"We're innocent!" The voice of one of the prisoners rang out over the clamor. It was the same small man with the long black beard I had seen in the kitchen of the jail in Tisza-Eszlar.

Bary nodded to Bako, who grabbed the man from behind and drew his arm across his throat, effectively cutting off his words.

"God help us, they're completely crazy!" Dr. Weltner shook his head.

"We have a witness to your horrible crime," Bary announced loudly. "Morris Scharf decided to tell the truth. His confession is signed and sealed. He watched through the keyhole of the lock on the front door of your synagogue as one of you did this terrible deed." He turned to Morris. "Is that what you told me, boy?"

Morris nodded his head. "Yes, I did."

I wanted to warn him not to say such terrible lies, but I was afraid to speak up.

"Louder!" roared Bary.

"Yes, that's what I say!" shouted the boy.

"My son! What are you doing? What are you saying?" cried Mr. Scharf. He held out his arms to Morris.

"Silence him!" Bary nodded at Chief Recsky, who motioned to his men.

Two gendarmes pushed through the prisoners and held Mr. Scharf's arms while Recsky took a filthy handkerchief out of his pocket and stuffed it into the man's mouth. Mr. Scharf garbled desperate noises.

"Morris Scharf, you confessed that the new butcher cut Esther Solymosi's throat and drained her blood into a pot," Bary said. "Point out to us the individual who did this horrible crime."

"The shochet! They're accusing the new shochet!" The lines of Jewish men broke as they looked at one another in horrified confusion.

"Back in line! Go on, boy. Show us this murderer!" said Bary.

Morris hung his head and shuffled between the rows of prisoners. One or two of them spat at him as he passed. He didn't raise his hands to wipe his face. He stopped in front of the bearded man who had spoken up before.

"Is that the man you saw murder the servant girl, Esther Solymosi?" Bary asked.

Morris nodded, stone-faced.

"Point him out to us!" Recsky commanded.

Morris slowly raised his arm and pointed his finger.

"Liar!" cried the man. "God is my witness that he is a liar!"

The other prisoners stared at Morris incredulously, afraid to make even the smallest noise.

Terrible grunts came from Joseph Scharf's mouth as he struggled to break away from the guards.

"And what is the name of the man who killed Esther Solymosi, the man you're pointing at?" Bary asked.

"He is Solomon Schwarcz, the new shochet." Morris's voice was little more than a whisper.

"Why are you telling such terrible lies? I did nothing! I'm innocent! I can prove it!"

Mr. Scharf's animal sounds as he strained against the guards were horrible to hear.

"The butcher killed the girl! The butcher killed the girl!" the villagers were shouting, waving their fists in the air. The clutch of Jewish women turned their heads away as if the words were blows. Even in the commotion, Morris did not raise his head.

"Silence!" Bary shouted. "Who were the men who held the girl down while Solomon Schwarcz cut her throat?"

Morris hesitated, then pointed to the two men standing on either side of Schwarcz.

"They help shochet kill girl," he said.

"What are their names?" Bary asked.

Morris shook his head and stared at the ground. .

"Who are you?" Recsky shouted. "What are you doing in Tisza-Eszlar?"

"I'm Abraham Buxbaum," said the taller of the two. "I did nothing! I came here to try out for the shochet's job. I didn't even know the girl!"

He wiped his forehead with the back of his hand.

"Why are you sweating?" Bary asked. "Are you nervous because you're guilty?"

"It's warm," Buxbaum answered. "Everybody sweats in the heat. I'm innocent!"

Bary's eyes rested on the shorter man.

"Who are you?"

"I'm Lipot Braun. I never saw the girl either. I, too, came to Tisza-Eszlar to apply for the shochet's job, but I was turned down."

"Who was chosen?"

Buxbaum and Braun looked at Schwarcz.

Bary smirked and addressed Morris.

"Only one more person to identify, boy," he said. "Tell us which one of the beggars lured Esther Solymosi into the synagogue?"

The beggars, barefooted in ragged clothes, were standing together among the other prisoners.

"Which beggar tricked Esther?" Bary repeated.

Morris lifted his head and looked around.

"He not here," he said. "Beggar not here."

"Are you sure?" Bary asked.

"I'm sure," Morris mumbled.

Bary gestured at the filthiest of the beggars.

"Could this be him? Is this the man you saw call Esther?"

Morris shook his head.

"Look again, boy!" Bary said. "Look carefully! Remember what we told you. I repeat – could this be the beggar who lured Esther Solymosi into the synagogue?"

Angry red splotches appeared on Morris's bruised face.

"Yes," he muttered, "it's that beggar."

"Louder, boy!" Bary said.

Morris nodded his head in the beggar's direction.

"It's him!" he said loudly.

"I wasn't even in your bloody town the day that servant girl disappeared!" cried the beggar. He took a step toward Morris. Two gendarmes grabbed his arms and pulled him away.

"What's your name?"

The man didn't answer. The gendarmes' hold tightened and Recsky raised his whip.

The beggar cringed. "Don't hit me! I'm Herman Vollner, but I swear with the All Mighty as my witness that I am innocent!"

"Kill the Jews! Kill the Jews!" The villagers were relentless in their hatred. I hadn't seen them this bloodthirsty since

85

the traveling puppet show, urging on Leslie the Brave to put an end to the Devil.

Bary turned to Morris with a self-satisfied smile.

"Did you tell your father you witnessed the murder of Esther Solymosi by looking through the keyhole?" he asked.

Morris remained mute.

"Talk, boy, talk if you know what's good for you!" yelled Recsky.

"Yes, I tell mein Papa what I see."

"What did your father tell you to do?" Bary asked.

Morris did not answer.

"Remember what I told you, boy," Peczely said softly. "Remember what I told you."

Morris clasped his hands over his mouth and began to rock on his heels.

"Papa say not tell anybody what I see. He say murder a secret." The words came out of him painfully, as if they had jagged edges.

"Point out your father to us!" Bary ordered.

Morris hesitated. Then he pointed at his father. Joseph Scharf closed his eyes.

Bary clapped Morris on the back. The boy winced.

"You did well, boy. Really well," Bary said.

Morris's face was blank. He looked like a stranger to me.

"Kill the Jews! Kill the Jews!" The villagers chanting was louder, frenzied.

Bary turned to the chief of the gendarmes.

"Mr. Recsky! Please order your men to escort the culprits back to jail. Tomorrow morning they will be transferred to the prison in Nyiregyhaza where they'll stand trial. We finally know who killed poor Esther Solymosi."

The gendarmes marched the prisoners away. Someone had freed Mr. Scharf from his gag. "Morris, my son, what are you doing? Have you taken leave of your senses?" His words were an anguished cry.

As soon as the gendarmes and the prisoners were gone, the rest of the Jews surrounded Morris.

"Liar!" A man charged at the boy.

"Traitor!" A tiny, bent woman tried to claw his face.

Bary laughed.

"Recsky, you'd better transfer the boy to the jail in Nyiregyhaza with the others," he said. "He won't last too long if we leave him alone with his brethren, and we need him hale and hearty as a witness. We'll find a safe cell for him."

After Morris was led away, I gathered up my pail to go back inside the prison. A couple blocked my way. It took me a moment to realize it was Pa and the yellow-haired woman. She was holding his arm possessively, Ma's shawl draped around her shoulders in spite of the warm May morning.

I couldn't let the chance go by. "Pa, have you heard anything from Aunt Irma? Is Clara well?"

He scowled as if he couldn't remember who Clara was. "What do you want from me?"

87

"Nothing, Pa! I don't want anything. I just want to know about Clara."

"Get away from me!" He moved to push past me.

The woman plucked at his sleeve.

"Peter, don't – it's your daughter, for God's sake!"

"Mind your own business!"

He shook off her arm and strode away. She shot me a sympathetic glance and followed him. I ran after them.

"Pa," I called. "Has there been word about Clara?"

He vanished into the crowd. A cold dread gripped me. Was something wrong with Clara? Was she dead? Is that why he wouldn't talk to me? I swore that I would somehow earn the money I needed to go to Csonkafuzes to see my sister. But soon I would have no job and no place to live. If I was ever to see Clara again, I had to think and think fast.

Gendarme Bako was leading the shackled Jewish prisoners to the horse-drawn cart waiting in front of the prison. Here was my chance!

"Please, sir," I begged him. "Take me with you."

"Why do you want to go to Nyiregyhaza?"

"I'm not needed here any longer. Sergeant Toth's housekeeper will be back in a few days. I need a job and I can get one in Nyiregyhaza."

He shrugged.

"Talk to Sergeant Toth. If he agrees, you can come."

—

CHAPTER II

THURSDAY, JUNE 1, 1882 – SATURDAY, JUNE 17, 1882

I knocked on the door of the office, my heart in my throat. I had slept under the stars for the past week. If I didn't get the job, I didn't know what I would do.

"Enter!" called a gruff voice.

I smoothed down my skirt, took a deep breath, and went into the room. Antal Henter, the warden of the Nyiregyhaza prison, was sitting at his desk. A gigantic white Komondor dog was lying on the floor by his feet.

"Come closer!" Warden Henter said, beckoning to me.

As soon as I took a step toward him, the dog lumbered to its feet and bared its fangs. It growled at me menacingly. I jumped backward.

"Steady, Felix! Steady, boy!" Henter said, scratching the dog behind its ear.

The dog shook its corded coat and sunk down to the floor.

"Gendarme Bako tells me that you worked in the jailhouse in Tisza-Eszlar," Henter said. "What were your duties?"

"I was Sergeant Toth's housekeeper."

Warden Henter was tall and handsome, and I was soon to learn that he was known for his good humor. He would slap his thigh whenever he told one of his many jokes. He stood up and circled me, looking me over with calculating eyes as if I were a horse he planned to buy. I wanted to disappear, to have the earth swallow me up.

"Well, you seem strong enough," he said. "How old are you?"

"Fourteen, sir."

"Teresa, the cook at the prison, needs a scullery maid to help her. You'll be paid the same as the girl before – and your room and board. You can sleep in one of the empty cells."

"Thank you, sir."

This was the best news. If I was careful, I could save enough for a train ticket to see Clara.

"Listen carefully!" Warden Henter continued. "We keep the Jewish prisoners who were brought to us from Tisza-Eszlar separate from the rest of the inmates. You are not to go near them under any circumstances. If you help Teresa distribute their meals, you will give their food to their guards, who will pass it on to them. If you have any questions, you may ask Gendarme Bako, who was transferred here. If you disobey my orders, you will be dismissed. Do I make myself clear?"

"Yes, sir."

"You may deliver the boy, Morris Scharf, his meals, but you are never to speak to him. Understood?"

I nodded.

"You may go now," he said, his handsome head already bent over some papers on his desk.

As I went, his dog's angry bark followed me.

Teresa was kneading dough to bake bread when I got to the kitchen.

"You're late!" she snapped.

"I'm a growing girl. I need my sleep," I said cheekily.

I knew that it was safe to joke with her. Over the last few weeks I had discovered that her bark was much worse than her bite.

She dusted off her hands before answering me.

"We're having visitors tomorrow. I heard that the Jews' lawyer is coming all the way from Budapest." She slapped the dough cheerfully.

"Yes, one of the guards told me about him."

"He'll be talking with his clients and with Morris too."

"I wonder what Morris will say to him. Do you think he was telling the truth?"

"Well, did they beat him?"

"They almost killed him."

"There's your answer. Mind you, you can't trust them Jews. Now take those two large pails of gruel to the prisoners." She gave the dough a half-turn and pounded it with her fist. "And remember, you're not to go into their cells."

The Nyiregyhaza prison was overcrowded and the inmates were very different from sad old Mr. Meszaros sleeping off a night of drinking in the jail back home. The inhabitants of the Nyiregyhaza prison ranged from petty thieves to murderers. Most of them were filthy, violent, and vulgar. On my first day, I had delivered the inmates' breakfasts right into their common cell. It took all of my wits and a skillful use of my knees and elbows to evade their groping hands and worse. Now I knew better. I always handed the pails to the guards in front of the cell and asked them to give the prisoners their meals. I wasn't about to make the same mistake twice.

"After you finish, sit down for a bite for yourself," Teresa said with a toothless smile.

I picked up the pails and I walked down the long narrow hallway leading to the cells. A guard met me at the end of the corridor and took the pails from me.

Back in the kitchen I filled a small tin container with Morris's meal. I waited until Teresa's back was turned and I slipped two biscuits from the batch cooling on a plate into the pocket of my apron.

I heard voices coming from Morris's cell. "Remember what I told you." It took me a moment to recognize that it was Mr. Bary speaking.

"It's not by chance, boy, that everybody hates Jews," he said. "The whole race is nothing but liars and thieves. But you, Morris, are different from the rest of your brethren. You are doing the right thing and you won't go unrewarded. If you help us, we'll set you up in a trade when all this is over."

"But I . . ."

"No, no," said Bary. "Don't say a word. Reflect on what I told you."

I heard the clanging of a key in the lock.

"Watch him, Bako," Henter's voice said to the gendarme standing guard in front of the cell. Both Bary and Henter walked by me, but I had learned that servant girls have the singular advantage of being invisible.

They'd be furious if they knew that I always talk to Morris when I deliver his meals.

I could see the melancholy expression on Morris's face through the bars of his cell. He brightened when he saw me. Bako opened the cell door. I went in and he locked it after me.

"I have to go take a piss," he announced. "I'll be back in ten minutes."

"I wondered when you were coming," Morris said. "Did you see my papa?"

This was the question he greeted me with every time I brought his meals.

"You know they won't let me see him. I can't even go into that part of the prison."

I took out a biscuit from my pocket to wipe the disappointment off his face.

"Thank you!" He tore it into pieces, then stuffed them into his mouth.

"The biscuits are fresh. Teresa just baked them. You'll never guess who they are for!"

He laughed.

"Tell me!"

"You're having a visitor tomorrow. He is coming all the way from Budapest"

His eyes widened. Besides his jailers, I was the only person he ever saw. He wasn't even allowed to visit his family. Bary said that he was kept under lock and key for his own protection and to keep him away from "harmful influences."

"Do you know who is coming?" Morris asked.

"I do, but first, have your breakfast. I'll tell you after."

He made a face at the sight of the gruel but transferred it to his own bowl and began to eat greedily. I sat down on the floor and leaned against the bars of the cell.

"How are you doing?" I asked.

He shrugged his shoulders.

"I'm all right . . . Recsky and Peczely went back to Tisza-Eszlar. Bary still comes to see me from time to time."

"What's Warden Henter like to you?"

"The same as the others, but at least there is only one of him and not three."

"I just noticed, your Hungarian is getting better."

"That's all I speak now, to the guards and to Henter and to Bary. Tell me, who is coming to see me tomorrow?"

"First, I have to tell you some good news and some bad news. Which do you want to hear first?"

"The bad news – let's be done with it."

"Sophie Solymosi wrote me a letter. Teresa read it to me. Sophie says that Bary and Recsky arrested more Jews in Tisza-Eszlar and then let them go after a few days."

An expression I couldn't identify flitted across Morris's face. "Julie, I hope you understand that I *had* to testify against Solomon Schwarcz and his friends and even Papa, in order to keep him safe. You know I had no choice. You understand that, don't you?" He worried a piece of thread on his sleeve. "They kept saying they would beat Papa and keep him in jail forever if I didn't confess."

He looked at me expectantly, but I didn't know how to answer. I occupied myself with gathering up the container in which I brought his food to him. I had to return it to the kitchen.

"Bary is insane," Morris said.

"He isn't the only one. Sophie wrote that there are people in parliament who are claiming the Jews are responsible for Esther's death."

"Has the world gone mad?" Morris's voice was full of desperation. He buried his face in his hands. "What have I done? What have I done?" He put down his bowl on his bunk and stood up. Then he began to pace the length of his cell. "Why do people hate us so?" he asked. "Why do they accuse us of such terrible crimes? Sometimes I wonder."

"Wonder what?"

He scuffed the toe of his boots along the clay floor of the cell and spoke without looking at me.

"Warden Henter keeps on telling me that all Jews are thieves and liars. That's what Mr. Bary and Chief Recsky say too. Can they all be wrong? I can't help wondering sometimes if we deserve their hatred?"

"My ma said there are good and bad people among the Jews, same as everybody else. I think she was right. When I sold eggs to the Jewish women, some of them were miserable to me and some were nice. Did you forget that your pa is a good man? What about the Rosenbergs? Look how kind they've been to Sophie! Dr. Weltner? He tried to cure my ma and gave her medicines to help her even though we had no money to pay him. I don't understand why so many people hate the Jews. I guess there are some people who need somebody to hate."

"Why?"

"I don't know why. Ask your visitor. He is supposed to be a smart man."

"You have to tell me who's coming."

"Here's the good news I promised you. His name is Karl Eotvos. He's the lawyer who's going to defend the Jews from Tisza-Eszlar. Mr. Heumann, their old lawyer, says that the trial is too difficult for him to handle alone. He'll be still helping with the case, but Mr. Eotvos will be in charge."

"Eotvos . . . It's not a Jewish name."

"He is a Christian. In fact, he's a nobleman."

"Then I don't understand why . . ."

I put my hand out. "Wait and hear what he has to say."

I took the second biscuit out of my pocket and slipped it into his palm, careful not to touch his hand.

"Eat this before somebody comes!"

"Delicious!" he said, gobbling it down. "You're a good friend to me, Julie. I wish I could give you a hug."

"Me too."

We grinned at each other shyly. Morris grew serious again. "I need your help, Julie," he said. "Tomorrow is my mama's yarzheit, the anniversary of her death. I want to pray for her soul and light a candle in her memory. Could you bring me a candle and matches?"

"My ma is also in heaven. You're lucky to have another mother."

His face darkened.

"I hate my . . . I forget how you say . . . not real mother."

"You mean, stepmother."

"Yes, that's what I mean. I hate her! She doesn't care about me. She only cares for Sam. I can't imagine what she thinks of me now."

"Don't say bad things about your stepmother. She is also your mother!"

"No, she isn't!" he said angrily. He sighed. "I wish my real mama was here. She would understand that I had to do what I did."

"I know in my heart that my dear mother is watching over me from heaven. Don't be scared. I'm sure that your mother is watching over you too. She won't let you come to harm."

Morris didn't reply. I stood up and smoothed my apron.

"I'll try to get some matches and a candle for you. If I can't find them anywhere else, I know that Warden Henter keeps both in his office."

"Be careful, Julie. I don't want you to get in trouble on my account."

—

CHAPTER 12

SUNDAY, JUNE 18, 1882

I dreamt of Clara again. She was crying for me. All the while that I was taking Morris his candle and matches and washing the dishes I could not shake the feeling I had to see her. How could I get to Csonkafuzes? I couldn't come up with a solution, but I did get a pounding headache. When I told Teresa I felt ill, she suggested I go for a short walk.

"I can spare you for a half-hour but not longer," she said. "There won't be church for you today. I still have a lot to do before the visitors arrive. I'll need your help."

I decided to walk down the lane running along the prison. The sun was shining outside and I started to feel better right away.

As I was passing under one of the barred windows set high up into the wall, I heard the sound of praying. I looked down the street. Nobody was in sight. A greengrocer's wheelbarrow piled high with watermelons had been left under the window. Its owner must have been making a delivery to one of the neighboring shops. I looked around again. The street was still deserted. I grabbed the edge of the wheelbarrow and climbed up on top of the melons. The watermelons rolled under my feet, so I tried to move as little as possible in order not to lose my footing. I was high enough to grab hold of one of the bars and to peek into the cell. I saw Morris below me. He had lit the candle I had given him and had put it on top of his cot. He was swaying back and forth in front of the candle with his eyes closed, murmuring softly.

I was just about to call down to him when Warden Henter appeared at the entrance to Morris's cell. The warden could be jovial, but it was frightening how quickly his smiles disappeared when he was alone with the prisoners.

Morris's eyes were tightly shut. He was so absorbed in his prayers he didn't notice Warden Henter's entrance.

"What do you think you're doing?" Henter shouted.

Morris jumped.

"I'm praying for my mama," he said. "Today is the anniversary of her death."

"A good thing too," Henter said. "One less Jewish bitch to cheat God-fearing Christian people!"

Morris lunged at him. The candle toppled over, spluttered, and went out.

"How dare you insult my mother's memory!" he cried. "Leave my mama alone!"

Warden Henter snickered like a schoolboy. He grabbed Morris's long forelocks and tugged on them with all his might. Morris was brought to his knees.

One of the guards appeared on the threshold of the cell.

"Warden Henter, you're wanted in your office immediately." Henter released Morris. The boy collapsed onto his cot.

I felt the watermelons under my feet begin to roll and I was falling.

"What's that noise?" I heard Henter ask.

I picked up my skirts and ran down the street as fast as I could.

Mr. Eotvos arrived at the prison in a fine carriage. He was a tall, imposing man. He was clean-shaven and formally dressed in city clothes with a black bowler hat on his head. He was accompanied by a smaller man, dressed in a similar elegant suit.

The warden greeted the men on the front steps of the jail with smiles and handshakes. They entered the building and headed to Henter's office.

"Hurry up! The warden wants refreshments served right away," said Teresa.

She bustled about the kitchen as she poured cool raspberry juice she had strained that morning into a pitcher. I put glasses and plates on a tray and a plate of biscuits beside them. I balanced the tray carefully on my way to the office because I didn't want the juice to spill over.

The visitors were sitting in armchairs while the warden was behind his desk.

"Ah, refreshments!" said Warden Henter. "You must be tired and thirsty after your long journey."

"Not at all," replied Mr. Eotvos. "Thank you, m'dear," he said when I put down the tray on a small pedestal table by his side.

I didn't know how to reply. No gentleman had ever thanked me before for my services. The door of the study was flung open. Gendarme Bako nudged Morris into the room.

"Our witness!" Warden Henter announced.

Morris was trembling. He gave a frightened look in my direction. I smiled back. I saw Mr. Eotvos looking at us.

"If you don't mind, Warden, I prefer to speak to the witness alone," said Mr. Eotvos.

"Certainly," Warden Henter said, a strained smile on his face. He stood up. "I have a busy day. Judge Korniss is waiting for me."

Mr. Eotvos's eyebrows shot upward.

"Judge Korniss? Was he appointed as presiding judge at the trial?"

The warden's face paled. He realized he should not have spoken.

"Yes, he was," he said lightly. "The judge and I have been playing whist together for many years – before all this nonsense started," he added before turning on his heels and closing the door firmly behind him.

After he was gone, Mr. Eotvos glanced at Bako.

"My instructions are to stay," said the gendarme.

Mr. Eotvos stared at him hard. Bako looked back, unblinking.

"If you must," Mr. Eotvos finally said.

I knew I should leave, but instead I retreated to the back of the room and began to dust the contents of a bookshelf with a corner of my apron. Just as I hoped, the men forgot I was there.

Mr. Eotvos walked up to Morris and ruffled his hair.

"You don't have to be scared of me, boy," said the lawyer. "I won't hurt you. I'm only here to meet you."

Morris raised his head, but he didn't look at him or answer him. He stared into the distance, as if he were in a kind of trance.

"What is your name, boy?" Mr. Eotvos asked.

Morris did not reply.

I finished dusting the bookshelf and began to polish a silver ashtray. I was afraid even to breathe as I didn't want to draw attention to myself.

"What are you called, boy?" the lawyer tried again.

Morris shot a frightened look at the gendarme at his side. Bako nodded his head grudgingly.

"I'm Morris Scharf," he finally said.

"Well, Morris Scharf, I am glad to meet you," said the lawyer, extending his hand. Morris didn't take it. Mr. Eotvos's arm dropped to his side, but his smile did not waver.

"My name is Karl Eotvos. At the trial, I'll be representing your papa and the other Jews from Tisza-Eszlar accused of this ridiculous crime. How old are you?"

Morris cracked his knuckles and wouldn't answer him.

"Tell me your age, Morris," said Mr. Eotvos.

Morris looked again at the gendarme beside him.

"Answer him," Bako grunted.

"Don't be scared. Mr. Eotvos won't hurt you," said the lawyer's companion.

"I'm almost fourteen years old," Morris answered.

"A big boy, almost a man." said Eotvos. "You're a good boy, aren't you? You love your family, don't you?"

Morris was biting his lips but remained silent.

"You love your father, don't you?" said Eotvos. "You also love your stepmother and little brother too?"

Don't be a fool, Morris. Don't say anything about hating your stepmother, I wanted to say to him, but I knew I had to remain silent.

"Yes, I love my family," Morris mumbled.

I let out such a loud sigh of relief I was afraid the men would hear me.

"That's all I wanted to know, boy," Mr. Eotvos said heartily, " . . . just your name and age."

He clapped Morris on the back. The boy winced. Mr. Eotvos looked thoughtful and lit a small cigar.

"Is there anything you want to tell me?" the lawyer asked. Morris shook his head.

Mr. Eotvos sighed and tapped the cigar.

"Then I have no more questions."

He turned to Bako. "Gendarme, you may take the boy back to his cell."

After Morris was led away, Mr. Eotvos turned to his companion.

"Poor boy," he said, "he is frightened out of his wits. I was afraid that he'd turn out to be a monster, but he is a terrified child, a victim as much as his father. Did you notice how he winced when I touched him? He is probably covered with bruises, but there is nothing I can do about it if he doesn't confide in me."

"A waste of time coming here." Mr. Eotvos's companion snapped closed his briefcase. "We accomplished absolutely nothing by meeting the boy."

"I beg to disagree with you, Andras," Mr. Eotvos said. "I have a good reading of the boy's character now. It'll prove to be invaluable in preparing our case."

The men picked up their fine gloves and their hats. As he was closing the door, Mr. Eotvos looked directly into my face. He gave a little nod, his lips parted in a half-smile. I had a feeling he wasn't surprised to see me in the room.

—

CHAPTER 13

SUNDAY, JUNE 18, 1882 – MONDAY, JUNE 19, 1882

The banging was so loud it woke me from the deepest of a dreamless sleep. I sat up and listened. The noise seemed to be coming from outside, at the front of the prison. I lit a candle and pulled on my skirt and blouse as fast as I could. I padded down the dim halls with a flickering candle lighting my way. The stone floor was cold beneath my bare toes.

Warden Henter was unlocking the front entrance of the prison when I got there. A boy a little older than me was standing on the steps. He was dressed in traditional peasant garb. Sweat was running down his face and he was breathing hard.

"What do you want?" barked the warden.

The boy bent over, trying to catch his breath.

"Is Mr. Bary here?" he gasped.

"He isn't staying in the jail, you fool!" said the warden. "What happened? Why do you want Bary?"

"They found a corpse at Csonkafuzes," said the boy.

"What corpse? Who found it? You're not making any sense!"

"A group of Jew rafters fished a corpse out of the Tisza River," said the boy. "It stank so much they buried it on the bank of the Tisza. When Chief Recsky found out what they did, he had them dig it up. The doc says that it's the body of a girl. Chief Recsky sent me to fetch Mr. Bary."

The warden grabbed the front of the boy's shirt and pulled him into the foyer.

"Did he say if it was the body of the missing servant girl from Tisza-Eszlar?" he asked.

The boy shrugged his shoulders.

"I don't know."

"You can go now," said the warden. "I'll send for Bary. He'll want to see the corpse in Csonkafuzes for himself."

Csonkafuzes was where Clara lived. I caught up with the warden as he was closing the door. He did not seem surprised to see me in a corridor in the middle of the night.

"Sir," I said, "could I please go with Mr. Bary to Csonkafuzes? My little sister lives there and I haven't seen her in a long time."

The warden looked confused, as if he didn't know who I was.

"I won't be gone long, sir. I haven't had any time off since I started working for you," I hastened to add.

He shook off my arm.

"You are from Tisza-Eszlar, aren't you? Did you know the missing girl?"

"Yes, sir. She was my friend."

"Bary might need you to identify the body, so you can go with him. Mind you," he said, wagging his finger, "you better come back as fast as you can or I'll be sending you packing!"

The door slammed shut behind him with a bang, but I barely heard it. I was already planning what I would say to Bary to make sure he would take me with him.

The next afternoon, the driver of Bary's carriage stopped to let me off on the outskirts of Csonkafuzes. "Remember, girl, you're here for a reason! You are to come to the river-bank as soon as you can." Bary's voice carried over the clop-ping of the horses' hooves as the carriage drove away.

A small boy was passing, herding a flock of geese, and I asked him if he knew my Aunt Irma. He laughed and said I was standing in front of Aunt Irma's house. It was tiny, no more than a room. The plaster was falling away in chunks and the stoop was muddy.

I knocked, but there was no sign of Aunt Irma. I picked my way through tall weeds to the yard behind the ram-shackle building without anybody seeing me. Clara was in the henhouse. She was taller and thinner than when I had last seen her six weeks ago. Her face was caked with dirt and her hair was matted. She was dressed in clothes Mama had made her, but now they were even smaller and more ragged. She looked just as she had in my dream.

She was collecting eggs from under the chickens and was so intent on her task she didn't notice me. The hens pecked at her stubby fingers, but she didn't seem to react to the pain.

"Clara!" I called. "Clara, it's me!"

She turned slowly with a frightened look on her face.

"It's me, Clara!" I repeated. "I've come to see you!"

The eggs dropped from her hands onto her bare feet. She ignored the gooey yellow mess and stared at me, her mouth open.

"It's me, Clara! Have you forgotten me?"

She flew into my arms. The frightened chickens began to squawk.

"I thought you'd never come!" she cried.

I hugged her as hard as I could and never wanted to let her go. We both began to cry.

"I want to go home! Take me home with you, Julie! Please, please, Julie, take me home! I want Ma!" she sobbed.

I sat down on the ground and pulled her into my lap, rubbing her back. Her bones felt delicate under my hands, like the bones of a little bird. She finally calmed down.

"What's wrong?"

"Aunt Irma, she is so mean to me," she said with a hiccup. "I'm always hungry. She never gives me enough to eat. If I do anything wrong, she beats me."

She held out her bare arms for my inspection. They were covered with black and blue bruises. I touched them gingerly, my heart breaking. I kissed the bruises and wet them with my own tears.

"Oh, my love, I can't take you with me today. I just can't. I have nowhere to take you to. I don't live with Pa anymore. I work at the Nyiregyhaza prison. My room is an empty cell. It's no place for a little girl. And don't you remember? Ma doesn't live in Tisza-Eszlar anymore. She went to live with the angels."

She nodded solemnly.

"I forgot," she mumbled. "I miss Ma so much!"

"So do I."

She burrowed her head into my chest and clung to me so tightly I was afraid she would squeeze all the breath out of me. Finally, I pried her fingers off my neck, lifted her off my lap, and stood up.

"I have to go now, but first I'll talk to Aunt Irma. She shouldn't be treating you so badly!"

"No!" She grabbed at my apron to hold me back. "If she finds out I told you she'll be mad!"

I patted her head.

"You're probably right. I won't say anything to Aunt Irma, but I swear to you I will come back for you as soon as I can and you and I will live together again."

"Just you and me and not Aunt Irma?"

"Definitely not Aunt Irma!"

I spit on a corner of my apron and rubbed her face with it, succeeding in streaking it even more with dirt.

"I have to go now," I repeated, "but I'll be back soon."

Her sobs wafted after me and she seemed so small standing in the center of the henhouse when I looked back. I vowed to return for her and to make a home for the two of us. I didn't know how I would do it, but do it I would, I swore to myself. That's what Ma would have wanted me to do.

CHAPTER 14

MONDAY, JUNE 19, 1882 –
FRIDAY, JUNE 23, 1882

Mr. Bary, Chief Recsky, Mr. Peczely, and Warden Henter were part of a buzzing crowd of people huddled around an object lying on the muddy bank of the Tisza River. The gorge rose in my throat at the sight of the hairless, naked figure of a girl. A small rag thrown over her midsection was the only concession to modesty. I quickly looked away. I had never even seen my own mother naked. A pile of clothes were on the ground close to the body.

A weeping Mrs. Solymosi was being supported by Esther's aunt. They were flanked by Sophie and her brother, Janos, and several people I recognized from the streets of Tisza-Eszlar. There was no sign of Morris or the shop-keeper Kohlmayer, the last person to have seen Esther alive.

None of the Jews from Tisza-Eszlar were present. There were also several strangers in city clothes. Standing apart from them was a group of men with worn faces, their heads covered by skull caps. They were the Jewish raftsmen who had found the body. Their rafts were moored on the riverbank.

"It's high time you got here!" cried Mr. Bary in greeting. "Look at the corpse carefully! Have you ever seen her before?"

I forced my eyes back to the wretched figure lying at my feet. I looked at the hairless head, the distorted face, the swollen throat, the defenseless body, and my heart filled with pity. I swallowed hard to keep my dignity and looked away once again.

Chief Recsky's fingers were suddenly like a vise around my cheeks as he forced my head in the direction of the dead girl. I closed my eyes.

"You better look if you know what's good for you," he whispered in my ear.

So I looked. I looked at the battered face long and hard. There was something familiar about the ravaged features. I looked even closer. Then I knew. My eyes traveled to the wretched girl's feet and rested on the crescent-shaped scar at the base of the big toe of her right foot. I had seen the same scar a thousand times before. I had no doubt in my mind.

"It's Esther, sir," I said in a quivering voice. "This poor creature is my friend Esther Solymosi."

Mrs. Solymosi flew at me, clawing at my face.

"Liar! Liar!" she cried. "This detestable lump is not my beautiful girl." She clutched Bary's arm. "A mother would know her own child, live or dead, wouldn't she, sir?"

Recsky pulled her away. Bary turned to me.

"You must be mistaken!" he said. "None of the others identified the body as Esther Solymosi!"

"No, sir, I'm not mistaken. With God as my witness, I'm telling you the truth. If you look hard you'll see that the body must have had Esther's features before she was buffeted this way and that by the river."

Bary shook his head. I could see by his expression he didn't believe me.

"Think carefully before you speak," Warden Henter warned me.

"Why do you keep on lying?" Mrs. Solymosi's voice was a screech.

I spoke as gently as I could.

"Look at her feet, ma'am! Look at the scar beneath the big toe on her right foot. Don't you remember when Magda stepped on Esther's foot when we were still young girls?"

"Hush your lying mouth!" cried Mrs. Solymosi. "That ugly lump can't be my Esther!" she repeated.

"Young woman, be careful what you say, for if you make a mistake, you'll have to pay for it," said Peczely in a silky voice.

One of the men in city clothes stepped forward.

"There is a way to settle this for once and for all!" he said. "Show this girl the clothes the corpse was wearing when the rafters fished her out of the Tisza. Show her the tin box full of paint the dead girl was clutching in her left hand."

"Silence, Zuranyi!" cried Bary. "The body can't be that of Esther Solymosi. The Jews cut Esther's throat! That would have left a scar."

All of us looked at the smooth, unmarked neck of the corpse on the ground.

"Use your reason, Bary," said Zuranyi. "If the dead girl was wearing Esther Solymosi's clothes, it must be her." He nodded at me. "If this girl was Esther's friend, she might recognize her clothes."

I tore my eyes away from the pitiful wreck and looked carefully at the garments on the ground beside her. I recognized Esther's red, white, and black plaid jacket. There was also her black skirt, white apron and blouse, and a white underskirt, the likes of which all of us wore. Beside it was the red-striped belt. On top of the clothes lay the same tin container I had seen in her hand the last time I had seen her.

"Those are Esther's clothes. She was wearing them the day she disappeared." I pointed at the belt lying in the dirt. "Esther never took off this belt!"

I fell silent before Chief Recsky's venomous glance.

"You see," said Zuranyi, "the dead girl must be Esther Solymosi. The clothes are hers. The blue paint in the tin box is more proof. You can't explain all this away."

"Esther told me she was going to buy blue paint at Kohlmayer's shop!"

Bary's face turned so red I was afraid he might have an apoplectic fit.

"The dead girl is not Esther Solymosi! This girl's throat is not cut and it is a fact that the Jews cut Esther's throat," he said. "The Jews must have taken Esther's clothing and put it on another corpse of similar age! They must have put the paint in this corpse's hand."

He marched up and down the riverbank, punctuating each step with a wave of his hand.

"Yes, that's what must have happened," he said. "The Jews put Esther's clothes on another body. This girl is definitely not Esther Solymosi."

Once again, all of us stared at the unblemished throat of the poor girl at our feet.

"How can you be so sure that the Jews killed Esther?" Zuranyi asked. "I beg you, Bary, be rational! This must be the body of the missing servant girl. Her friend recognized her. She was wearing Esther's clothes. She was clutching blue paint in her hand. Her friend says she has the same scar at the base of her toe as Esther did. What are the odds of two people having the same scar in the same spot?"

"You're wrong, Zuranyi!" Bary said. "I know that the Jews killed Esther Solymosi because I have a witness. A Jewish witness."

Poor Morris, I said to myself.

—

CHAPTER 15

WEDNESDAY, JULY 19, 1882 - THURSDAY, AUGUST 24, 1882

I was sitting under the kitchen window, sweltering. Perspiration matted my hair and ran down my cheeks and my back. I kept wiping my hands on my apron as I was afraid my damp palms would leave sweat marks on the shirt I was mending.

After I had visited Clara in Csonkafuzes, I realized it would take me forever to save up enough money from my salary to have Clara come and live with me. I had to come up with a plan to earn extra money. My head was full of hare-brained schemes that couldn't work until I noticed a few days later that one of the prison guards was missing several buttons from his jacket.

"I'll sew on the buttons for you, sir," I offered.

To my surprise, he accepted and pressed a shiny coin into my hand. After I gave him back his jacket he told his cronies I was a good seamstress. Since then, the prison guards had kept me busy with britches that had to be patched and torn shirt sleeves that had to be sewn together. I kept the little pile of money I earned tied up in a handkerchief in my apron pocket in the daytime and under my pillow while I slept. When my fingers closed around the small bundle, I thought of Clara and the day when we would be reunited.

The hot weather took my breath away and I stopped to fan myself with my apron. I wiped my face and my hands again and then it was back to work. Despite the heat, I took my time and made my stitches nice and even, like Ma had taught me. My mind wandered back to Csonkafuzes. Since that day by the river I couldn't stop thinking about what I had seen there. Nobody could convince me that the corpse the raftsmen fished out of the Tisza was not Esther. I had tried to explain, over and over again, what I knew to Mr. Bary, but he wouldn't listen to me. He told me to mind my own business. He even ordered my poor friend's body to be dug up from her grave for a second time to be examined by learned city doctors who said they couldn't decide for sure whether the dead girl was Esther. I knew better.

When I found out that Bary would not relent, I went to see Warden Henter. I found him in the prison courtyard throwing a stick to his dog.

"Bring me the stick, Felix!" he cried.

The beast lumbered after the stick and fetched it for him every time.

"Good dog! Good dog!" he said, scratching Felix behind his ear.

I stood silently, a few meters away, waiting for him to notice me.

"What do you want?" he finally said.

The dog began to growl. Warden Henter patted his head.

"It's all right, boy," he murmured.

The dog calmed down and Warden Henter turned back to me.

"Have you got something to say?" he asked.

I told him why I was certain that the corpse from the river was Esther. He listened carefully, steepling his fingers. "You talk too much," he said evenly when I finished. "If you persist on repeating your nonsense, I'll have to find somebody else to help Teresa in the kitchen."

I realized at that moment that although I knew the truth, nobody around me wanted to know it. Mr. Eotvos, the only person who would have listened to me, was far away in Budapest.

I saw that the sun was overhead, so I put my mending aside and carefully packed up Ma's workbox. Teresa was at the shops, but she had told me before she left to warm up the potato soup she had prepared for the prisoners' lunch and to deliver it to them. I carried the two pails of soup to the guards and asked them to give it out. As usual, I left

Morris's meal for the last. I hadn't seen him since I went to Csonkafuzes. An extra crust of bread was hidden in my pocket, next to the coins. I planned to slip it to him while Bako wasn't looking. I had also put away a bone for the warden's dog.

I was on my tiptoes as I passed the warden's office on my way to Morris's cell. Felix was lying in front of the door with his eyes closed. He must have sensed my presence for he climbed to his feet, growling. This time I was prepared. I took out the bone from my pocket and threw it to him.

"Down, doggy! Down, doggy!"

The beast fell on the bone ferociously. I passed him as quickly as I could, my heart pounding.

When I got to Morris's cell, I found him sitting on his cot with his head resting against the wall. I thought he was asleep. The tiny room was unbearably hot. Bako, standing guard in the hall, opened the metal doors to let me in. Morris looked up at the clanging of his key.

"I'll lock you in with the Jew boy for a few minutes while you give him his soup," Bako said. "I want to get something to eat myself." He snickered. "Don't get too close to the dirty Jew. He stinks too much!"

Morris and I watched him turn the corner.

"It's good to see you, Julie."

I sat down on his cot, next to him. It's never easy to apologize, but it had to be done:

"I owe you an apology, Morris, for doubting you when you told me your pa and your people were innocent. I should have believed you."

"You're loyal, Julie. Thank you."

I moved farther away from him. "I may be loyal, but there is something that's been troubling me for a long time. I think about it every time I see you. I don't understand how you could have testified against your own pa and your friends when you knew they are innocent?"

"They beat me! Can't you understand that? I couldn't take it anymore!" he cried. "They told me that they'd beat my papa too and keep him in jail forever if I didn't sign their confession. What else could I do?" He grasped his head with his hands. "What else could I do? What else could I do?"

I wanted to comfort him, but I couldn't. His lies had brought about so much wretchedness and there would be more to come.

"Why do you believe me now about the girl?"

"They found Esther's body in the river at Csonkafuzes. I have proof that you Jews didn't kill her, but nobody will listen to me."

"Proof? What kind of proof?" he asked eagerly.

"Eat your lunch first. It's easier to think on a full stomach."

He drank down the soup greedily and ate the bread. He sighed. "That was good. I was so hungry."

"I'll try to slip something extra to you at suppertime."

"Do you think you can? Be careful, Julie."

I told him that I recognized the poor battered face of the dead girl fished out of the Tisza.

"She was Esther. She wore the same clothes that I saw Esther wearing the day she disappeared. She had the same scar at the base of her right toe as Esther did. She was even clutching a tin of paint in her hand. Esther told me that she was going to Kohlmayer's to buy blue paint the last time I saw her."

"You're sure?"

"I've never been more sure of anything in my life. The body at Csonkafuzes was Esther's body. The Jews were supposed to have cut her throat. Esther's throat didn't have a single mark on it. I tried to tell Mr. Bary, but he won't listen. Nobody wants to hear. I don't know what to do."

"You must tell my papa what you told me. He'll make Bary listen. My papa is a very smart man."

"You know that I can't get close to your father. He and the other Jewish prisoners are guarded day and night."

"I understand. I keep telling myself that at least my papa isn't alone. He has his friends with him. Do you think they can convince Mr. Bary?"

"Morris, we know that's never going to happen. The person who has to know is Mr. Eotvos. I think he'll believe you, but he is far away."

He sidled closer to me. "You must tell him the truth when he comes to town for the trial."

"I will."

"You're a good friend, Julie, the only friend I have."

I remembered Esther saying the same words to me the last time I saw her alive. They frightened me.

"Are you all right, Morris?"

"All right? How could I be all right?" he said angrily.

The violence in his voice made me cringe. "Hush! Keep your voice down!"

"How could I be all right?" he whispered. "I never leave the jail. I never see anybody but you or my jailers. I haven't seen my family for months. I'd go crazy without you to talk to." We heard the steps of the guard down the hall, so we fell silent.

The next morning, Teresa asked me once again to deliver breakfast to the prisoners. When I got to Morris's cell, it was empty. One of the guards told me he had been released from the prison. However, he wasn't allowed to go home to his stepmother and brother. He would be living in Warden Henter's house, under the care of the warden.

CHAPTER 16

SATURDAY, SEPTEMBER 23, 1882 – SUNDAY, NOVEMBER 19, 1882

I had used up all of the white thread in Ma's workbox and there were still four more of the prison guards' shirts to darn before the sun set. It was Saturday, so the Jew store near the prison was closed. I had to go to Kohlmayer's in the Old Village, even though the trip would use up precious hours of freedom. I had no choice.

As I hurried along, I recalled that Esther's last errand was also to Kohlmayer's. Esther must have walked the same route I was taking. What sad thoughts had filled her head as she followed the dirt road? My thoughts were interrupted by a carriage passing so close to me I thought it would run me over. I flattened myself against the building beside me. The carriage's wheels deflected a stone that hit my leg. Then the vehicle came to a halt.

I shook my fist at the driver.

"What do you think you're . . ."

I fell silent when I recognized Warden Henter in the front seat. Next to him was another figure. The passenger's wide-brimmed hat shaded his face. It wasn't until he glanced at me that I saw that it was Morris, but a very different Morris from the one I remembered. Gone were his long forelocks. His dark skull cap, black trousers, and white shirt with fringes had been replaced by the wide pantaloons, sturdy boots, vest, and hat with a tall crown worn by Hungarian boys.

Morris stared at me blankly with eyes like black pebbles. Only the muscle that began to twitch at the corner of his mouth betrayed that he had recognized me.

I turned my head away from his empty eyes. Warden Henter didn't even look at me.

He pulled on Morris's arm. "What's the matter, boy?" he asked. "Haven't you ever been to the county archives?" He pointed at the building behind us.

"No, sir, I haven't," mumbled Morris.

The warden patted him on the back.

"Come, my boy, let me prove to you that you will be amply rewarded for describing the killing of Esther Solymosi," he said in a matter-of-fact tone that made the hair on the back of my neck stand up.

He pulled Morris's arm through his own and the two of them entered the building. Morris shot a frightened look in my direction before the door slammed shut behind them.

I waited a second before I followed them into the building. Nobody paid attention to me as I followed their voices up the staircase to a large room divided by a wooden counter with cabinets behind it. I hung back but I could clearly see Morris standing in front of the counter, still as a statue. Warden Henter was leaning over the counter and whispering into the ear of one of the clerks behind it. The man chuckled.

I noticed a bucket of water and some rags in a corner of the room. I got down on my hands and knees and began to wash the marble floor, careful at the same time to keep my face away from Warden Henter.

"I can do that!" the man said. He tapped the side of his nose and then turned to a young clerk behind a desk at the side of the room.

"Hey, Fritzi! Bring me document 523D."

"You want a document from the D file? But those are dea – "

"Never mind what they are . . . just give me the document!" interrupted his colleague.

The youth shrugged his shoulders.

"Suit yourself," he mumbled as he ambled over to one of the cabinets. The drawer was full of papers. The man pulled out a sheet from the center of a file and handed it to his colleague, who held it out to Warden Henter.

"Here is the letter from the Minister of the Interior you requested, Warden," the older clerk said solemnly. His lip was trembling as if he was trying to suppress laughter.

Warden Henter took the letter from him and read it carefully. "I was right, Morris," the warden said. "The minister has stated in an official letter that if you help us convict the Jews of Tisza-Eszlar of Esther Solymosi's murder, the government will pay for your apprenticeship in any profession of your choosing after the trial is over. I would advise you to do your training away from your hometown." He cleared his throat. "I hope you realize you can't go back to your family, not after what you testified."

"I know, sir, I know." He held out his hand. "May I see the minister's letter, please?"

"Absolutely not!" cried the warden. He handed the letter back to the older clerk. "This is an official document, forbidden to civilians! Surely you do not doubt my veracity?"

"Of course not, sir," said Morris.

"Well, our business is done here. It's time to go." The warden nodded at the clerk.

"Glad to be of service, sir," said the clerk.

While they continued talking, I flew down the stairs and hid behind a pillar.

"You are very fortunate, Morris, that I am a generous man," Warden Henter was saying as they came out of the building. "I'll make sure that the minister honors his promise to educate you," he added, his back to me. Morris was blinking in the sunlight and he gave a start when he saw me. I shook my head.

Morris started back into the building.

"Where do you think you're going?" the warden cried.

"I forgot my water jug upstairs in the office," Morris said. "I'll go and get it."

"Stay where you are!" the warden barked. "I'll go!"

He bounded up the stairs. Morris turned to me.

"Go!" he said. "Get out of here!"

"What are you going to do if you can't go home?"

"Henter will be back in a moment. Go!"

"But what will happen to you? I want to talk to you."

"Not now! Come to Henter's house tomorrow, an hour after church. That's the only time I'm left alone. Go to the back gate. It's set into the fence. I'll let you in. Nobody will see you. The yard is next to a meadow. Now leave," he said, "while you still can!"

It was unseasonably warm. The trees in their red raiment looked like torches in the sunlight. Father Gabor's sermon had lasted forever and Sunday was Teresa's day off, so I had to return to the prison after church to heat up the midday meal she had prepared for the prisoners. By the time I delivered it to the guards for distribution, there was no time left to eat if I wanted to get to the warden's on time. My stomach was complaining.

Nobody was in sight when I arrived at the large, gracious building. I turned down the lane running beside the stone fence and followed it to the very end. If Morris hadn't told me about it, I would have missed the gate, for it was overgrown with ivy. I lifted my hand to rap on the door when I heard voices.

"Remember, my son, that without Christ, there is no salvation. You must believe in Christ in order to be saved. Unbelievers will burn in hell for all eternity. Do you understand me?" I didn't recognize the voice, but it sounded clear and sure.

"Yes, Father, I do." Morris's response was firm.

"I will go now," the man said, "but I want you to reflect upon what you heard in church today and what I told you. I will be back later to continue our catechism lesson."

There was the sound of feet crunching on the dead grass followed by silence. I waited a few moments before knocking on the gate. It swung open immediately. Morris grabbed my arm and pulled me into the garden.

"I was waiting for you!" he said. "I didn't know if you'd come."

"I was afraid the priest would come back."

"Oh, you don't have to worry about Father Paul. He is a nice old man. Bary and Henter want me to become a Catholic. They asked Father Paul to teach me. The old man always takes a nap after lunch. He won't be back for a while." He sighed. "It's the only time I'm left by myself."

He led me to a table and two chairs that had been set up on the grass. In addition to a Bible, a pile of documents, and a bottle of ink, there was a plate of cookies and a pitcher of milk on the tabletop.

"Sit down," he said. "Here. Eat something." He pushed the plate toward me.

I lowered myself gingerly to the edge of one of the chairs and reached for a vanilla crescent.

"How can you be so calm, Morris? They'll see from the house that I'm here and then we'll be in trouble!"

"Those block the view," he said, pointing to a row of tall chestnut trees between the house and the table.

I reached for another cookie. Morris poured me a glass of milk.

"If nobody watches you, what stops you from going home? Your family would forgive you."

"No, they wouldn't. I can't go home. Everybody knows what I did. You understand that I had to do it, don't you?" He had said this to me and to himself so often that the words had almost lost their meaning.

I couldn't give him the reassurance he was seeking because I truly didn't understand.

"Why don't you tell your papa what happened? A lot of people have been hurt by what you did."

"I can't talk to him, Julie. Papa is still in jail. I guess you know that." He sounded close to tears. "They broke their promise and didn't let him go. I haven't seen him for months. I miss him so much, and Sam too."

"You're in Henter's good books now. Why don't you ask him if he'd let you visit your father?"

"I have, but Papa doesn't want to see me. Henter asked him over and over again to let me visit, but Papa says I am no longer his son." He closed his eyes to the sun. "The Jews must have poisoned him against me. They're evil, you know."

"How can you say that? How can you be so sure that Warden Henter is telling you the truth? Has it occurred to you that perhaps he didn't even ask your father if he wanted you to come?"

Morris's face was so fierce I drew away from him.

"Don't say bad things about the warden! Maybe he's got a bad temper, but he treats me like a son. He'd never lie to me."

"He insulted your mother!"

Morris's voice was cold. "He didn't know her. He didn't know that she was different from them."

"Them?"

"Never mind." He ran his finger across the rim of his glass over and over again. "Let's not fight, Julie. You're my only friend besides Henter. Promise me that you'll come and see me again?"

All through that warm late fall I met Morris every Sunday after church. He was lonely, I knew, and there were always good things to eat. Besides, I was curious. The weather turned cold in mid-November. Morris was waiting for me in the garden despite the icy wind. He was sitting bundled up at the wrought-iron garden table, trying to keep the newspaper in his hand from blowing away.

"We'll have to find somewhere else to meet. It's too cold outside," he said, blowing on his fingers.

"What are you doing?"

"My homework. The warden gives me this newspaper and then we discuss what I read."

He shook his head.

"It's full of horrible news. Look at this headline."

He handed me the paper, but I gave it right back.

"You know I can't read. Tell me what it says."

He read aloud:

"'Jews Kill Christian Girl.'"

I dropped the newspaper as if it had burned my fingers. The wind riffled the pages, but Morris grabbed it.

"It's called *The Independence*," he said. "The warden says that it's the best newspaper in the country because it's not afraid to tell the truth. It says that the Jews killed Esther and put her clothes on another dead girl's body."

He waved the pages at me.

"You have to be smart to write for a newspaper. Bary and Henter believe every word that's written in *The Independence*."

"Morris! You know that your pa and his friends are innocent. You told me that you confessed because they beat you and you wanted to save your pa!"

"They could have killed her without my knowing."

"How can you say that? You know better than anybody that your pa and his friends did nothing wrong. The body I saw was Esther. How can you believe these lies you are told?"

I grabbed *The Independence* out of his hand and tore it in half.

"I don't know what to believe anymore. Can everybody be wrong?"

"They must be because I know they didn't kill Esther."

I struggled to find the right words. "Don't listen to Bary and Henter, Morris," I said. A heavy hand grabbed my shoulder. I jumped. Morris stood up, knocking his chair over. The pages of the newspaper scattered on the ground. Warden Henter dragged me to my feet. His dog began to bark.

"What are you doing here?" he asked, furious.

Felix clamped his jaws on the edge of my skirt. I could hear it rip.

"Whoa, boy! Whoa! Let go!" the warden said.

The dog stepped back, slobbering.

"Why are you here?" the warden said.

Morris tried to answer for me.

"It's not Julie's fault, sir. I invited her."

"I'll deal with you later!" he said to Morris. He clenched my chin in his great paw of a hand.

"Aren't you the wench who works in the kitchen at the jail?"

"Yes, sir."

"Get out! If I ever see you here again, you can bid your job good-bye!"

I ran to the garden gate. My heart was still pounding when I found Teresa warming her hands at the kitchen's brick hearth.

The next Sunday, after church, I went back to the garden. The trees were bare and the sky was a grim pewter. I rattled the iron gate, but it remained closed. I tried again the next week. The week after that it snowed during the night. I knew there was no point in going to the garden anymore.

I sometimes saw Morris riding about town in Warden Henter's carriage. He was never alone so I couldn't speak to him. He would give me a sad little smile or wave after a quick glance at the warden. As the weeks passed, he stopped doing even that.

—

CHAPTER 17

TUESDAY, JANUARY 23, 1883

"You've been in a mighty bad mood these last weeks." Teresa was plucking a chicken, a job that always made her cheerful. "Bako's got some business with that Sergeant Toth in Tisza-Eszlar. Why don't you ask him if you can go with him?"

"Are you sure you can spare me, Teresa?" She waved a feathery hand in response and gave me a toothless smile. "You're no good to me moping around. Do you good to see your pa and your friends."

I didn't tell her that a visit with my pa was the last thing I wanted, but I knew that no matter how many britches I patched or how many shirt sleeves I darned, my little hoard of coins was growing very slowly. Clara wouldn't survive until I had enough money to fetch her. I was ready to risk

Pa's wrath and try again to reclaim the wages Sergeant Toth had handed over to him.

It was a cold January day and I bundled up as well as I could. How I wished that I still had Ma's warm shawl! I told myself not to be silly and I wrapped the new shawl I had made out of an old blanket around my shoulders. Bako stopped the horse-drawn buggy in front of my old home.

"I'll meet you here in two hours. Be here or you'll be walking back to Nyiregyhaza!" he said before driving off.

The cottage looked even shabbier than I remembered. The whitewash was streaked and piles of dirty snow covered the sad, dead remains of Ma's garden. But this had been my home. I had suffered Pa's fury here, the slam of his knuckles, the bite of his harsh words. And it was where I had felt my ma's love and her kindness. Everywhere I looked I could see Clara as she used to be, when she would confide her baby secrets and ask me to make the hurt go away when she scraped her knee.

I knocked on the door, but there was no answer. I knocked louder. The yellow-haired woman was clinging to the doorframe as if for dear life. She reeked of drink. Her hair stood up in clumps and her skirt was covered in stains.

"What'cha want?" she asked.

"I'd like to speak to my pa."

"Ain't here."

Despite her desperate grasp of the doorframe, she started to slip to the floor.

"Where is Pa?"

She snorted. "Your guess as good as mine! Try the Three Bulls!" She caught herself just as her feet gave way, pulled herself up, and slammed the door in my face.

I stood at the closed door. I knew that I had no choice. Who knew when Pa would get home? I couldn't wait, not if I didn't want to miss my ride back to Nyiregyhaza. I would have to tackle Pa in the public house.

The street to the tavern ran past the synagogue. Two gendarmes were leaning against the building, chatting and chewing tobacco, but if they were supposed to be guarding it, they were not succeeding. All the windows were broken. The windows of the Scharfs' house next door and several neighboring houses had also been smashed. There was broken glass everywhere. Even Dr. Weltner's home had a patchwork of wooden boards in the windows.

The blind eyes of the buildings and the crust of shattered glass on the ground made the street look like a dream of something both familiar and dreadful. There was more to the sense of emptiness: the children with long forelocks who used to play in the street and the men in dark suits and hats who used to bustle about their daily business were gone. The Jews of Tisza-Eszlar had disappeared.

I approached one of the gendarmes.

"Excuse me, sir, I am from another town. What happened here? Where are the Jews?"

I was afraid he would hear the hammering of my heart.

The gendarme spat on the ground.

"They're gone!" he said.

"Gone? What do you mean?"

"Once they realized that we didn't want them here, they left Tisza-Eszlar." He stubbed out his cigarette. "Do you want to see what their church looks like now?"

He stood aside and I went into the building. The prayer books had been thrown on the floor. Someone had torn most of the pages out of them. The white pages with strange script blanketed the clay floor like snow. I picked up a book. I tried to smooth out the remaining pages in it but then I dropped it. There were too many pages missing.

A malevolent hand had taken an ax to the pews. Fragments of wood were everywhere. The walls were full of muddy handprints. Excrement in a corner gave off a foul odor. I could hear the scritch-scratch of mice behind the walls.

The gendarme appeared in the doorway.

"Seen enough?" He looked at my stricken face. "Girl, are you one of them?"

"Of course not!" He looked so menacing that I quickly added, "I don't even like Jews!"

"Good riddance, I say!" He spat on the floor of the synagogue.

I came out into the cold winter sun. I was shaken, and the thought of talking to Pa was more dispiriting than ever.

A bit of windowpane tinkled to the ground from the Rosenbergs' deserted house as I passed it. Mrs. Solymosi lived around the corner. Perhaps Sophie was staying with her. I longed to talk to a friend.

For a moment Mrs. Solymosi didn't recognize me, but when she did she barred my way. Her face twisted in hate.

"Liar! How dare you come here? What do you want?" she shrieked, pushing me away. I stumbled off the stoop.

"Mrs. Solymosi, please let me in. Please let me talk to Sophie."

For the second time that day, a door was slammed in my face.

The single, small window of the tavern was so filthy with smoke that, despite the bright day, the room was gloomy. It took a few moments for my eyes to accustom themselves to the dark. Pa was at the back of the room, surrounded by farmhands. They were shouting with laughter. Tall tankards of ale stood on the table in front of them.

I wanted to run away, but I forced myself to walk up to Pa. I shoved my hands into the pockets of my apron so that he wouldn't see their trembling. Pa's companions fell silent and stared at me, but Pa didn't look up.

"Hello, Pa, it's me, Julie."

Pa took a deep swig from his ale, but kept his eyes on the table.

"I have to talk to you, Pa."

With effort he lifted his head. I stepped back at the menace in his eyes. I felt as if I was going to vomit. I wanted to turn on my heels and run away but stood my ground when I remembered my little sister's sad face.

"Can I talk to you in private, Pa?"

"What do you want?"

I clenched my fists. The pain from my nails digging into my palms steadied me and cleared my head. I spoke as fast as I could, desperate to get out the words.

"It's Clara, Pa. Aunt Irma is starving her. She looks sick and she's miserable. I can take care of her, but I need money for that. I know Sergeant Toth gave you my wages. Could you spare me a portion of them?" I was begging. "She's only a baby, Pa. Ma would hate to see her so neglected."

I heard the sudden intake of the breath of the men at the table, but none of them said a single word. Pa rose from his seat and pushed his face so close to mine I could smell the sourness of his breath.

"So you want money?" He raised his hand and pushed me away. I lost my balance and fell to the floor. "How dare you!" he roared. "It's not money you'll be getting from me!"

I picked myself up to the sound of jeering laughter and forced myself to move slowly as I walked to the door.

—

CHAPTER 18

TUESDAY, MAY 15, 1883

Trial fever had hit Nyiregyhaza. The date of the trial of the Jews accused of killing Esther Solymosi was set for June 19, 1883. Every housewife embarked on a feverish cleaning of rooms they planned to rent out to the hordes of newspapermen and onlookers expected to descend upon the town.

For days I had been scuttling between the courthouse and the prison while Teresa peppered me with instructions. We were to provide food and drink for the lawyers during the trial.

I was carrying salt biscuits in a wicker basket when I saw an agitated crowd milling in front of the courthouse. I burrowed into their midst and asked a woman what was happening.

"The Jews' lawyer will be arriving any moment," she said. "I want to get a look at him."

Hardly were the words out of her mouth when a carriage pulled up in front of the courthouse. The crowd fell silent. Two men were sitting in the carriage. One of them was Mr. Eotvos. Next to him was the same companion he had brought with him to the Nyiregyhaza prison to interview Morris. Mr. Eotvos gave a little smile and waved to the crowd. Several people waved back. ·

"My but he's a fine gent," said the woman beside me.

"Jew lover!" a rough-looking man in bricklayer's clothing shouted.

"Why are you helping the Christ killers?" A woman in an embroidered kerchief shook her fist.

An object whizzed by my ear. Mr. Eotvos stumbled, hitting his shoulder against the wall of the building. His friend grabbed his arm and prevented him from falling to his knees. I noticed that the sleeve of Mr. Eotvos's elegant jacket was torn.

The lawyer stooped and picked up a large stone lying at his feet. The two men examined the stone calmly, ignoring the cries of the crowd. "Go home, Jew lover!" "Go home! Go home!" Mr. Eotvos placed the stone back on the ground and the men walked with measured, dignified steps, into the courthouse.

I took the biscuits to the temporary pantry we'd set up and laid them out under a clean cloth. Gendarme Bako was in the corridor. He was dabbing his neck with a handkerchief. I hung back, not wanting to push past him.

Mr. Eotvos pulled off his gloves thoughtfully. "Why weren't there gendarmes outside to protect us?"

"Judge Korniss said nothing about protection."

Mr. Eotvos gave Bako a long cool look but didn't respond. He fingered the tear in his jacket.

Bako, red-faced, motioned to me. "You, girl, I want you to mend the gentleman's coat." Here was my chance to tell the lawyer what I had found out on the bank of the Tisza in Csonkafuzes.

Bako led us to a small room off the hall. Mr. Eotvos remained silent until the door closed behind him. He turned to me.

"So, young lady, we meet again," he said.

I nodded.

"What is your name?" he asked.

"Julie Vamosi, sir. I can repair your jacket so the tear will barely show."

Mr. Eotvos smiled. "Never mind my jacket. I'm more interested in what you have to say. I last saw you at the Nyiregyhaza prison, didn't I, when I was interviewing Morris Scharf?"

"Yes, sir. I was there. I was cleaning the room while you were talking to Morris."

"Yes, I remember." His eyes twinkled. "You're a resourceful young woman."

"Yes, sir."

"Am I correct in thinking you might want to help Morris?"

I finally gathered enough courage to look him in the face.

"I've been wanting to talk to you for a long time, sir. But I don't understand. I thought you were helping the Jews. Morris is helping Mr. Bary."

"Morris is lying." He sounded matter of fact. "You know that. If I can clear his father of this ridiculous accusation, I'll also be helping Morris."

I tried to follow what he was saying, but he was using a formal kind of Hungarian that almost sounded like a foreign language.

"I'm trying to understand Morris, to discover why he isn't telling the truth. I think that you know why. I want you to tell me."

I couldn't decide what to say, so I stood mutely.

The lawyer began to pace the small room, deep in thought. He stopped in front of me.

"Let me make it easier for you. Just nod your head for a yes or shake your head for a no to answer my questions. Can you do that?"

"Yes, sir, I can."

"Have you ever seen Morris beaten?" he asked.

I remembered Morris lying senseless on the floor of the jail in Tisza-Eszlar. I remembered Warden Henter beating him in his cell when Morris lit a candle in memory of his mother. I remembered everything. I nodded my head.

"Have you ever heard Morris threatened?"

I nodded again.

"Was Morris forced to accuse his father and the Tisza-Eszlar Jews of killing Esther Solymosi?" asked Mr. Eotvos.

I remembered how Peczely warned Morris that his father would be tortured and kept in prison forever unless Morris confessed. Again I nodded.

Mr. Eotvos patted my shoulder.

"You're a good girl, Julie," he said. "You see, Andras. It's just as I thought. The boy was tortured. Poor Morris. Unfortunate boy. He is nothing but Bary's marionette, a puppet he is using to implicate the Jews."

The relief at being believed made me feel light-headed. The words couldn't leave my mouth fast enough.

"There is more, sir. Mr. Bary and Warden Henter only allow Morris to see them and Father Paul. He can't visit his family. I used to see him on the sly, but I can't anymore. I know that Mr. Bary and the warden are constantly telling him that the Jews are evil, wicked people. They tell him day and night, and Morris is starting to believe them because there is nobody there to tell him different. They keep saying that the Jews will harm him if they ever get their hands on him. They tell him that the Jews will never forgive him for testifying against them. He is becoming afraid of his own kind!"

"None of this surprises me." He looked out at the street below, empty now.

"It's all being done for nothing, sir."

"What do you mean?"

"I know for sure that the Jews are innocent. I have proof."

He grasped my arm so tightly I winced. He must have noticed my distress because he let go.

"I am sorry. Please, tell me all you know."

Once again I recounted the story of the scar at the base of the toe of the corpse fished out of the river at Csonkafuzes.

"Sir, I recognized her. The dead girl was Esther. Her face was all but destroyed by the water, but I could still tell it was Esther. Mr. Bary showed me the clothes the dead girl had been wearing. They were the same clothes Esther had on the day she disappeared. When they found her, she was clutching the tin container Esther took to Kohlmayer's to buy the paint. Esther had a scar at the base of her big toe and so did the dead girl – the same scar, in the same spot. That wouldn't be possible for two different people. There is no doubt in my mind that the dead girl is Esther. And sir, there wasn't a single mark on Esther's throat. The Jews couldn't have killed her."

"Did you tell Mr. Bary?"

"Yes, sir. And also Warden Henter."

"And they didn't believe you." Mr. Eotvos exchanged a grim look with his friend, then patted me on the shoulder again.

"No need to worry any longer. It is not up to you to make them listen. That's my job now."

The bells of the church across the square rang twelve times. I knew I had to return to the prison.

"Please, sir, I must go." Teresa would not be pleased if she had to prepare the midday meal alone.

Mr. Eotvos reached into his pocket and took out a coin.

"No, sir! I don't want your money. I'm happy that you'll make everything right again. Please help Morris! I know he did a terrible thing, but still –"

"I'll do my best." Mr. Eotvos gave me a tight little smile.

He pressed the coin into my palm.

"Take the money. It might be useful some day."

When I reached the street, I looked at the coin the lawyer had given me. It was a whole forint. It brought me that much closer to Clara.

CHAPTER 19

TUESDAY, JUNE 19, 1883

"Please, Teresa, please let me go! I don't want to miss the beginning of the trial. Morris will be testifying today. I want to hear what he has to say."

She stopped stirring the pot of goulash she was cooking for Warden Henter's dinner. "That well may be, missy, but who'll do your work?" She punctuated her words with stabs of her wooden spoon. "I don't have the time to do your work and mine."

"I'll do it! I'll work all night if I have to. I'll still scrub the floor and wash the dishes. I'll have the potatoes peeled before I leave. I'll do everything you want me to do if only you'll let me go! And I promise, I'll be back before lunch to help you."

She put her hands on her ample hips, an expression of mock consternation across her worn features.

"You better or I'll, I'll . . ."

She burst out laughing.

I ran up to her and gave her a big hug.

"Thank you! Thank you!"

She pushed me away, but I could see that she was pleased.

"Be careful, Julie," she said, suddenly serious. "If the warden sees you at the trial, it might cost you your job. I'd hate to see you gone!"

"He won't see me. There'll be lots of people there."

She shook her head.

"Don't say I didn't warn you. Well, I can see it's no use talking to you." She waved her wooden spoon in the air. "What are you waiting for? If you're going to go – go! Get out of here or you'll be late!"

The streets of Nyiregyhaza were teeming with visitors for the trial. The cafés and taverns were full and there wasn't a single room to be let.

I was desperate to see the trial, but not if it meant using any of the money I was saving for Clara for admission. Fortunately, with all the errands I'd had to run for Teresa, I had grown to know the courthouse well.

The day the trial started the steps of the courthouse were crowded with disappointed ladies and gentlemen, dressed in their holiday best, who had been turned away for lack of room. There were dozens of armed gendarmes among them. I turned the corner to the side of the building.

The lane running beside it was empty. I stopped in front of a narrow door set into the wall. It was always kept open for tradesmen delivering their wares. I slipped into the courtroom.

At first, a pillar obscured my line of vision. I peeked around it cautiously. The front entrance was guarded by two armed gendarmes. A table and chairs had been set up on a platform in front of me. Three gentlemen sat behind the table. I recognized Warden Henter's whist partner, Judge Korniss, in the middle seat. He was dressed formally in his judge's robes. Next to him were two other gentlemen, also in robes.

To the left of the judges' table I spotted Mr. Eotvos's burly figure and bald head. Next to him sat Mr. Heumann, the Jewish prisoners' original lawyer, and three other gentlemen. I realized that all of them must have been attorneys for the defense. Across from them, to the right of the judges' table, were the prosecutors. I had heard that they were also from out of town. Beyond the prosecution and defense lawyers' tables was an open area that held benches awaiting the defendants. Chairs had been set up behind them for officials. Mr. Bary, Mr. Peczely, and Chief Recsky were sitting there. Warden Henter sat next to them. On one side of the platform a table had been set up for the court stenographer and on the other side sat Mrs. Solymosi, all in black, and her lawyer.

The rest of the courtroom was taken up by rows and

rows of chairs filled with a motley assortment of county dignitaries, elegantly dressed gentlemen, rough laborers in their field clothes, and reporters with their notebooks open. A door behind the judges' platform was open, and through it I could see ladies rustling about in their brightly colored summer silks. I was the only girl among all the men, but with my rough red hands and my apron I was less conspicuous there than I would have been among the fine ladies. I stayed in my spot behind the pillar.

I looked around me and recognized many of the faces. I had seen them often enough strolling the streets of Tisza-Eszlar while I delivered eggs or ran errands. But there were no Jews among them. Teresa had told me that only eight Jewish people of the two thousand who lived in Nyiregyhaza were allowed to get tickets to the trial. With a jolt I recognized Pa in a row of rowdy men who'd clearly already made a stop at the tavern. He didn't turn around, so I was quite certain he hadn't noticed I was there.

I forced myself to leave the protection of the pillar and sat down in an empty chair in the last row.

The gentleman in the seat next to mine sniffed. I knew that I smelled of the onions I'd chopped for the day's goulash.

To my relief, he lost interest in me when Judge Korniss banged his gavel on the felt-covered table.

"Attention!" He rose to his feet. "Let us begin. I am Judge Korniss and I will be presiding over these proceedings. I am the judge who'll be doing all the talking. My esteemed colleagues are the Honorable Erno Gruden," he said, nodding at the judge on his right, who smiled graciously, "and the Honorable Barna Feher is to my left." Dour-faced Judge Feher inclined his head solemnly. "The three of us will review the facts presented before the court at the end of the trial. Judges Gruden and Feher will cast the votes that will determine the outcome of this case. As presiding judge, I will vote only if my two colleagues cannot agree upon the verdict.

"I would also like to introduce the prosecutors, Mr. Szeyffert and Mr. Lazar," he nodded at the men on his right. "The defense will be represented by Mr. Eotvos, Mr. Heumann, Mr. Funtak, Mr. Friedmann, and Mr. Szekely." He gestured to the table on his left.

Finally, he addressed a gendarme standing guard beside the podium.

"Deputy, bring in the defendants."

A shabby line of men in handcuffs shuffled into the room. As they passed Mr. Bary's seat, he stared at them venomously. They were dressed in black suits or black caftans. Their heads were covered with skull caps, and white fringes were hanging below their suit jackets. Each of them had long sideburns and beards. One of the men seemed familiar to me. I realized he was Morris's father, although a wizened and much older Mr. Scharf after fourteen months of captivity. Next to him was the butcher Solomon Schwarcz and the three other men Morris had picked out from the lineup of Jews in front of the synagogue in Tisza-Eszlar.

The prisoners settled down on the benches as Judge Korniss rose again and began to speak.

"We are here today to delve into the mystery surrounding the death of young Esther Solymosi, who disappeared from her hometown of Tisza-Eszlar on April 1, 1882. You can be sure that we will leave no stone unturned to discover what happened to this young girl, still really a child. If the defendants are found guilty of this heinous crime, they will be severely punished. If they are found innocent, their liberty will be restored to them."

He pointed to the prisoners huddled in their seats.

"I shall now read the charges against the defendants. Stand up, Solomon Schwarcz, Abraham Buxbaum, Lipot Braun, and Herman Vollner!"

The three butchers and Vollner, the beggar, dressed in filthy rags, struggled to their feet. Mr. Eotvos also stood up from his seat at the defense table.

"Defendants, face me," ordered the judge.

The prisoners seemed bewildered, as if they were moles emerging into daylight.

"You, Solomon Schwarcz, Abraham Buxbaum, Lipot Braun, and Herman Vollner, are charged with first-degree murder in the death of Esther Solymosi, a resident of Tisza-Eszlar. How do you plead?"

"Not guilty, Your Honor." Mr. Eotvos's voice rang clear. "My clients maintain their innocence."

"These prisoners may take their seats," ordered Korniss. "Stand up, Joseph Scharf."

There was more clanging as Mr. Scharf rose. Mr. Eotvos again stood up.

"Turn toward me," said the judge.

The prisoner faced him.

"You, Joseph Scharf, are charged with complicity in the death of Esther Solymosi of Tisza-Eszlar. How do you plead?"

"I'm innocent!" cried Mr. Scharf. "I've done nothing!"

"Silence!" Judge Korniss brought his gavel down. "Be quiet! You'll have your chance to talk during the trial."

"We're sorry for the prisoner's outburst, Your Honor," said Mr. Eotvos. "It won't happen again. The prisoner is emotionally upset. We plead not guilty to the charge."

"Your plea is noted," said Judge Korniss. "However, your client had better learn to obey the rules of this court or he'll live to regret his behavior!"

"We understand, Your Honor," said Mr. Eotvos mildly.

"The prisoner may sit down," barked the judge.

He poured himself a drink from a jug on the table. I saw Mr. Scharf look longingly at it while the judge downed his glass.

"During the next part of the proceedings, the prosecutors will present their case," he continued.

He paused while a clock above the podium rang eleven times, reminding me that I had to go back to the prison to help Teresa. I was determined to return in the afternoon in time for Morris's testimony.

I stood up quietly, afraid even to breathe. I must have made more noise than I realized because after I pushed the door open and looked back over my shoulder, I locked eyes with Pa's malignant gaze for the instant before the door swung shut behind me.

—

CHAPTER 20

WEDNESDAY, JUNE 20, 1883

I was settling into my seat when Morris was led into the courtroom. The first thing I noticed was his pallor. He was dressed like a Hungarian boy in a white-striped sailcloth jacket with his feet shod in sturdy peasant boots. He stopped abruptly in front of the judges' table, but he kept his eyes fixed on the floor. He clutched the handrail of the judges' platform. A rush of noise filled the courtroom, excited, angry whispers from the rows of men and loud Yiddish words that sounded like curses from the prisoners.

"Silence in the court!" cried Judge Korniss, banging his gavel. "I will not tolerate such disorder in my courtroom!" He turned toward Morris, a cold smile creasing his face. "What's your name, son?" he asked.

"I'm Morris Scharf."

"You'll have to speak louder. The court must be able to hear you. How old are you?"

"I'll be fourteen on July 11."

"Are you the son of Joseph Scharf, the beadle of the synagogue in Tisza-Eszlar?"

"I am, sir."

Judge Korniss leaned over the table until he was almost nose to nose with Morris.

"I must advise you, son, that you are not obligated to testify against your father."

Morris cast such a quick glance at Mr. Bary that I almost missed it. Bary was leaning forward in his chair, his elbows on his knees. He was flanked by a solemn Mr. Peczely and Chief Recsky, whose mouth had twitched into a half-smile. Warden Henter was beside them. He looked bored.

"I want to testify," Morris mumbled.

I heard the hiss of a sharp intake of breath from the row of prisoners.

"Please let the court note that the witness was advised of his right to refuse to provide testimony against his father," said Judge Korniss. He turned to Morris. "You spoke several times to Investigating Magistrate Bary about the disappearance of Esther Solymosi, did you not?"

"Yes, sir."

"What did you testify?"

"In the beginning, I said nothing," said Morris.

"You changed your tune when Chief Recsky interrogated you, didn't you?" asked the judge.

"Yes, sir."

"What did you tell Chief Recsky?"

"At first, I told him and Mr. Peczely nothing, but later on I confessed." Morris's shoulders were hunched around his ears. "I decided to tell the truth."

"Why?"

"Chief Recsky told me that I would remain in jail forever if I didn't tell the truth. He said that I would be also a prisoner of my conscience for perpetuity if I didn't reveal what I knew. So I confessed – of my own free will."

"What did you say in your confession?" Judge Korniss asked.

Morris began to recite his confession in a monotone. His stiff manner reminded me of the way the puppet Leslie the Brave had given his speeches in the traveling puppet show I had seen in Tisza-Eszlar.

"On the first day of April in the year 1882, the Jews of Tisza-Eszlar congregated for their Sabbath prayers in their synagogue," said Morris. "There were some strangers among them – Solomon Schwarcz, the new ritual butcher, and the two other unsuccessful candidates for the ritual butcher's job. I didn't know their names at the time. They were those two defendants sitting there," he said, pointing at Lipot Braun and Abraham Buxbaum.

"Prayers started at eight o'clock or eight-thirty in the morning and ended just after eleven o'clock. The Jews left the synagogue, but Solomon Schwarcz and those two stayed behind." He pointed once again at Braun and Buxbaum.

"That's a lie!" cried Braun, a small man with a luxurious beard.

Again, the noise in the courtroom rose.

"Let the boy talk!" ordered the judge.

The onlookers fell silent.

"I myself left the synagogue for my father's house. Before lunch, my father and a Jewish beggar man who stayed with us over our Sabbath" – he nodded toward poor Herman Vollner, slumped on the defendants' bench – "They called the girl into our house to move a candelabra from one table to another. Jews are not allowed to do such tasks on the Sabbath.

"A few minutes later, this beggar Jew asked Esther Solymosi to go into the synagogue with him, telling her they needed her help to carry something out of the synagogue."

"That's not true!" Vollner struggled to get up.

"Be quiet!" yelled the judge.

The men next to him tried to calm him.

"Continue your testimony, son," said the judge.

"I followed Vollner and the girl but stayed farther back, out of sight. About fifteen minutes had passed when I heard screaming and moaning coming from the synagogue. I ran up to the door, but I found it locked so I peeked through the keyhole. I could see the small covered area that leads into the sanctuary clearly. I saw that the defendants Buxbaum and Braun were holding down the girl on the floor. Solomon Schwarcz cut her throat and drained her blood into an earthenware pot."

Pandemonium broke out. Judge Korniss beat the table with his gavel, but he could not contain the shouting and cries.

"Not a word is true!" said Buxbaum.

"God will punish you for such lies!" shouted Braun.

"Silence!" roared the judge. "Silence or I will clear the courtroom!"

"The Jews consumed my daughter!" cried Mrs. Solymosi. Her face was twisted in agony.

"My good woman, please control yourself!" said prosecutor Szeyffert, his distaste written on his face.

"Continue, Morris," ordered the judge.

"I don't know what the butchers did with the corpse of the servant girl. I was afraid of being discovered, so I went home. My family was still eating their lunch. I was gone for less than an hour."

Mr. Eotvos stood up, straightened his tie, and nodded at Morris as if he were a gentleman passing in the street.

"What time do you claim to have seen the crime committed?"

Morris eyes darted to Bary, Recsky, Peczely, and Henter.

"What time do you claim to have seen the crime committed?" Mr. Eotvos repeated.

Morris shrugged his shoulders.

"I don't know . . . It had to be shortly before noon because the sun was not yet overhead."

Mr. Scharf jumped up from his seat, the clattering of his handcuffs almost drowning out words that seemed to be dragged from his very heart.

"Morris, my son, have you lost your mind? Do you want to see me executed?"

Two deputies pushed him back onto the bench.

The onlookers were yelling again.

"Brave boy, to tell the truth!" A man at the back of the room waved his handkerchief.

"Down with the murderers!" This time it was a young man wearing a floppy silk cravat and a rose pinned on his lapel.

Once again, Judge Korniss banged his gavel. Morris looked as if he were about to take a bow in front of an audience. He drew himself up to his full height and smiled. The gentle boy I had known had disappeared.

"Son, you claim you don't know what the accused did with the girl's body?"

"No, sir, I don't. I imagine they threw her into the Tisza River," Morris answered in a loud voice.

The defendants were shaking their heads.

"Did you memorize these lies, my son?" cried Mr. Scharf. He stood up again.

"I humbly beg to address the court." The gendarmes stepped back. Mr. Scharf made a ragged noise, deep in his throat. "I cannot bear to listen to my son wanting to see me killed!"

"What do you mean?" asked the judge. "Your son didn't accuse you of murdering the girl!"

"I'm no different from the other prisoners. If he accuses them, he is accusing his own father!"

The judge leaned toward Morris once more.

"Son, do you know the Ten Commandments? Do you know that you're not supposed to bear false witness against your fellow men?"

"Yes, sir. I know that."

"Do you maintain that your testimony is the truth?" continued the judge.

"I do, sir. I'm telling the truth."

"What about honoring your father and your mother?" Solomon Schwarcz lunged at Morris and was pulled up short by his handcuffs.

He spat into Morris's face before the deputies could stop him. Morris turned red as he wiped his face. The guards pushed the butcher back onto the bench.

"I'm telling the truth! You cut the girl's throat!" Morris said to Schwarcz angrily.

"I will not have such an exhibition in my court! Your clients will pay dearly for it!" Judge Korniss said to Mr. Eotvos. He turned back to Morris. His poisonous gentle words made me sick.

"Son, do you still maintain that your testimony is given of your own free will? Did Chief Recsky threaten you to get you to testify?"

Morris, the tips of his ears burning, shot another quick glance in Recsky's direction.

"Chief Recsky never threatened me. He never laid a finger on me."

Recsky's smile broadened. Mr. Eotvos approached the judge.

"Judge, may I address the witness?"

"You may."

"Thank you, Your Honor."

Mr. Eotvos said nothing for a moment. Then he shook his head.

"Can you tell us your testimony in verse or perhaps in German?"

Morris remained silent.

Mr. Eotvos faced the judges.

"Your Honors, may I address the court again?" asked Mr. Eotvos.

Judge Korniss nodded.

"Your Honors, the defendants would like Morris Scharf to repeat his testimony in German. They believe he was coached in Hungarian. The boy's Hungarian was not good at the time Esther Solymosi disappeared. Nor would a simple Jewish boy know some of the words he is using – *defendants, testimony, perpetuity* are words he would not normally know."

"I refuse to speak German! Or Yiddish!" cried Morris. "I only want to speak Hungarian!"

"The witness must be permitted to testify in the language of his choice," said prosecutor Szeyffert.

"The prosecutor is right." The judge pursed his lips. "The boy must be allowed to speak in the language he chooses.

However, he will address the defendants. Face the defendants and look them in the eye as you repeat your testimony," he ordered Morris.

Morris turned toward the prisoners' bench and the wretched men sitting there. "On the first day of April in the year 1882, the Jews of Tisza-Eszlar congregated for their Sabbath prayers in their synagogue. There were some strangers . . ."

"Your Honor," interrupted Mr. Eotvos, "it's obvious the boy was coached. He is repeating his testimony word by word."

"I was not coached," said Morris stubbornly. "I'm telling the truth."

"Let the boy finish!" ordered the judge.

Morris repeated his testimony once again, not changing even a single word.

"Liar!"

"Why are you doing this?" rang from the defendants' corner.

Lipot Braun stood up.

"May I address the witness?"

"You may," said Judge Korniss. He pulled his pocketwatch out from beneath his robe and scowled. "Make your point quickly," he said.

Morris looked at Braun contemptuously, without blinking an eye.

"I have a question for you, Morris," said Braun. "What did I do?"

"I already told you what you did."

"Repeat it to me," said Braun. He looked around at the other defendants.

"You and Buxbaum made the girl lie down on the floor in the synagogue, and then the two of you held her down while Solomon Schwarcz cut her throat," Morris repeated flatly.

Braun stepped closer to Morris and the boy shrank away from him.

"Your Honor, the defendant is trying to intimidate the witness!" interjected prosecutor Szeyffert.

"Keep your distance!" said Korniss.

"Sorry, Your Honor," said Braun, stepping away from Morris before addressing him once more. "You dare say to my face that I held down the girl?"

"You did! You and Buxbaum held her down."

"Where was I holding her?" asked Braun.

"What do you mean?"

"Which part of her body was I holding?" Braun asked.

Morris blushed deeply. "I don't remember."

"Once, you told Investigating Magistrate Bary I was holding her leg, and another time you told him I was holding her head. So what was it – the head or the leg?" He didn't wait for an answer before he sat down.

Mr. Eotvos sprang up from the defense table.

"Your Honor, it's obvious the witness is lying. He keeps changing his story."

"I'm not lying! I can't remember whether the defendant held the girl's leg or her head. But I saw him and Buxbaum hold her down on the floor while Solomon Schwarcz cut her throat and drained her blood into a pot. And that's the truth!"

Mr. Scharf jumped up and tried to run at Morris. The guards caught him and pushed him down.

"I have had enough of the prisoners' nonsense for today!" Judge Korniss signaled to the gendarmes. "Take them back to their cells."

The line of prisoners was led out of the courtroom while the onlookers jeered.

"We will resume our proceedings tomorrow morning at ten o'clock sharp," announced Judge Korniss over the din.

I slipped out of the courtroom while the onlookers were struggling to their feet. Warden Henter passed me at the bottom of the courthouse steps.

"What are you doing here, wench? Don't you have enough work to keep you in the kitchen?"

"I was just curious . . ."

"Well, don't be! You have no business here. If I see you at the trial again, you'll regret it!"

I ran back to the prison, thinking of all the news I had for Teresa.

—

CHAPTER 21

THURSDAY, JUNE 21, 1883

The next morning, I washed the dishes and drew water before Teresa was satisfied she could do without me. By then she was as eager as I was to see me off. "Hurry along, girl, and don't forget a single thing they say!"

Mr. Eotvos was already cross-examining Morris by the time I got to the courthouse. I sat on the floor behind a pillar. I hoped that it would hide me both from Pa and Warden Henter. I could see what was going on if I craned around it. There was no sign of Pa, and the warden was at the other end of the hall, so I began to breathe more easily.

Morris was dressed in the same clothes as the day before. However, gone was any vestige of the shy, awkward boy. He stood up straight and spoke confidently.

"Yes, sir," he said boldly in answer to a question Mr. Eotvos must have asked just before my arrival. "Yes, sir, I understand the charges against my father and the other defendants."

"Tell us, boy, how do your parents treat you? Are they good parents to you?" asked Mr. Eotvos.

Morris glanced in his father's direction before responding.

"Sometimes they're kind to me, but a lot of the time they yell at me and punish me. My stepmother doesn't take good care of me. She doesn't love me. She only loves my brother, Sam. She beats me sometimes and so does my father. Of course I haven't lived with them for fourteen months."

Mr. Scharf jumped up from his seat.

"Morris, my son, how can you say such things? You've had nothing but love!"

Morris appeared transfixed by the painting of the Emperor that hung on the wall, but he did not answer.

"Counselor, warn your client to be quiet or I'll have him removed from the courtroom," Judge Korniss thundered. "He'll have his opportunity to question the witness shortly."

Mr. Eotvos walked over to Mr. Scharf, put his arm around the distraught father's shoulders, and whispered something into his ear. Mr. Scharf sat down. "My client regrets his outburst, Your Honor," said Mr. Eotvos. "He assures me that it won't happen again."

He turned back to Morris, smiling at the boy.

"I have a few more questions for you, boy. Who spoke

to Esther Solymosi and asked her to come into your house when you saw her pass under your window? Was it your father?"

"No, sir, it was me."

"You called her into the house? Why?"

"My father told me to."

"What happened after the girl moved your candelabra off the table?"

"The beggar Vollner, who was staying with us, asked her to accompany him to the synagogue. He told her that something had to be carried out of there."

Vollner shook his head violently but remained silent.

"Let me change the topic, Morris," Mr. Eotvos said. "You testified that you saw the murder of Esther Solymosi through the keyhole of the lock on the door of your synagogue?"

"Yes, sir, I did."

"You testified that Braun and Buxbaum held down the victim while Solomon Schwarcz cut her throat and drained her blood into an earthenware pot. Is that correct?"

"It is," Morris said warily.

"Who held the pot?" asked Mr. Eotvos.

"What do you mean?"

"Who held the container into which Esther Solymosi's blood drained?" repeated Mr. Eotvos.

The onlookers in the courtroom leaned forward, on the edge of their seats.

"Solomon Schwarcz held the pot," For the first time, Morris sounded uncertain. "He cut the girl's throat with one hand while he held the pot with his other hand."

"Once the victim's throat was cut, did the blood pour out smoothly into the pot or did it come out in spurts?" Mr. Eotvos's gory question was delivered in a confiding way, in the same tone he would use to discuss the weather.

Morris's face turned crimson.

"I don't remember," he said.

"How can you not remember?" Mr. Eotvos shook his head, mildly puzzled. "You claim you were watching the murder through a keyhole. You must have seen how the blood poured out."

"It flowed smoothly into the pot that Solomon Schwarcz was holding," Morris said.

"Was the girl's clothing stained by the blood?"

"No, sir. Solomon Schwarcz was holding the pot very carefully"

"That's strange," said Mr. Eotvos. He walked up to the defense table and picked up a sheet of paper with writing on it. "This is an affidavit signed by three distinguished physicians," he said, waving the paper in Morris's direction. "All three maintain that if a person's throat is cut, and the person expires as quickly as you claim that Esther Solymosi did, a major artery must have been severed. This must have caused the blood to gush out of her throat like a geyser, splattering everything in its path – the clothing of people standing close to the victim and the floor and the walls next to the victim." I felt faint. He was talking about Esther, my Esther, who loved her red-striped belt and the riverbanks and her mother and her sister and her brother.

"Explain to us how is it possible that Esther Solymosi's blood flowed smoothly into the container?"

"I just remembered. The blood was everywhere," stammered Morris.

"That is an important detail to forget," said Mr. Eotvos. One bushy eyebrow quirked.

"Well, I did forget it. I have a lot on my mind," Morris said defiantly.

"Let's talk about what you *do* remember," said Mr. Eotvos. "How long were you looking through the keyhole?"

Morris looked at Mr. Bary as if waiting for directions. Bary and Recsky stared back at him with impassive faces. Morris didn't answer.

Mr. Eotvos repeated the question. "How long were you at the keyhole?"

"Three-quarters of an hour to an hour," stammered Morris.

"If you were standing there for an hour observing somebody being murdered, why didn't you call for help?"

Morris looked at Bary again before he replied.

"The street was empty. There was nobody I could call for help."

"If you say so."

Morris pulled his shoulders back and stuck out his chin.

"I *do* say so! I'm telling the truth!"

The atmosphere in the courtroom crackled with tension.

"Calm down, boy," said Mr. Eotvos. "I have a few more questions for you. I'm certain that you, as well as I, want the truth to come out."

"I already told the truth!" said Morris. "Solomon Schwarcz cut the girl's throat and Braun and Buxbaum held her down."

"That's what *you* claim!" said Mr. Eotvos in a dry tone. "Miss Farkas, the sister of Tisza-Eszlar's magistrate, and young Elizabeth Sos told Mr. Bary that your little brother, Sam, claims that it was your father who called Esther Solymosi into your synagogue, where he held her head and you held her leg while Solomon Schwarcz cut her throat."

"That's a lie! They bribed Sam with sweets. Sam is only five years old. He'll say anything for a piece of candy! Mr. Bary knows I'm telling the truth."

"Ah, Mr. Bary and his truth!" said Mr. Eotvos.

"Counselor, be careful of your remarks or I'll have to hold you in contempt," warned the judge.

"I'm sorry, Your Honor. I was carried away by the heat of the moment. No disrespect was meant toward my esteemed colleague. I have just a few more questions for the witness."

He turned to Morris.

"You testified that after you witnessed Esther Solymosi's murder, you returned to your parents' house and found your father, stepmother, and brother eating lunch."

Morris nodded.

"What were they talking about?" asked Mr. Eotvos.

"What do you mean?"

"What was your family talking about over their meal?"

"I don't remember," said Morris sullenly.

"Your memory seems to be getting worse," said Mr. Eotvos. "Did you tell your parents what you saw through the keyhole at the synagogue? Did you tell them about Esther Solymosi's murder?"

"I did."

"What did they say?"

"My stepmother told me to be quiet. My father ordered me not to tell anyone what I had seen. I did as they asked me to until I decided to do the right thing and told Mr. Bary what I knew."

"This concludes my examination of the witness," said Mr. Eotvos. "Let the court note the witness's hostile behavior. I'd like to reserve the right to recall this witness for further questioning at a later date if need be."

"The court agrees," said Judge Korniss.

Mr. Scharf beckoned to Mr. Eotvos. Mr. Eotvos bent to confer with the prisoner. "My client, Joseph Scharf, would like to question the witness." Mr. Eotvos squeezed the man's shoulder.

"The court grants permission," said Judge Korniss.

"Thank you, Your Honor," said Mr. Scharf as he approached Morris.

"Morris, you must look the defendant in the eye while you testify," ordered the judge.

Father and son faced each other. Mr. Scharf's expression was full of sorrow and Morris's face was full of defiance. His eyes were fixed on his father's shirt collar. Mr. Scharf held out his hand. "Do you remember who I am, Morris?"

"Why do you ask me such a foolish question, old man?" snapped the boy.

"My son, I know you studied Torah, and it was my hard-earned money that paid for those studies," said Mr. Scharf. "Tell me, my boy, do you know the Ten Commandments?"

"I already told the judge that I do."

"What is the second commandment?"

"'Honor thy father and thy mother.' We already talked about that," Morris said sullenly. "Old man, what do you want from me? I have said everything I have to say. Indeed, I have to return to my home and finish the work my teachers have left for me."

"How do you know such words as *indeed?*" asked Mr. Schwarcz. "You must have been coached in your testimony, my son. No one knows better than me that your Hungarian is not good."

Morris snorted.

"I have *not* been coached! I studied hard and now I speak Hungarian fluently.

"Repeat to me what you told Mr. Bary when he asked you what happened to the girl," said Mr. Scharf.

"I already told Judge Korniss what I saw. I don't want to have to say it again!"

"The law requires you to cooperate with your father," said Judge Korniss.

"Your Honor, the witness isn't looking his father in the eye," interjected Mr. Eotvos.

"You were already instructed to look at your father," said the judge.

Morris lifted his gaze reluctantly and began his recitation: "On the first day of April in the year 1882, the Jews of Tisza-Eszlar congregated for their Sabbath prayers in their synagogue. There were some strangers among them – Solomon Schwarcz, the new ritual butcher, and the two other unsuccessful candidates for the ritual butcher's job . . ."

Not a single word of Morris's testimony differed from what he had originally told the court and what he had repeated to Braun and Buxbaum. The three testimonies were identical.

"Son, you speak as if you were reading your words from notes," said Mr. Scharf. "Tell me, where was I while you were observing this murder through the keyhole?"

"You were at home, eating lunch in our house."

"Why didn't you come and get me? We live next door to the synagogue."

Morris shrugged.

"I don't know why."

"Why didn't you tell me of the crime you witnessed?" asked Mr. Scharf.

Morris looked at his father defiantly.

"I did tell you after I returned home, and you told me never to mention it to anyone ever again."

Mr. Scharf stepped closer to him.

"My son, my son. Where is my son?" He began to tear his own hair. "What are you saying? What are you saying?" His words were little more than a whisper. Everyone fell silent as he approached the judges' table.

"Your Honors," he pleaded. "Please help me! I beg you! First, my five-year-old Sam was bribed with sweets and frightened into telling lies. When he proved to be too young to be a reliable witness, the state used my poor Morris to attack me!"

Judge Korniss banged his gavel. "You're out of order! Keep your sickly imaginings to yourself or you'll pay dearly for it! You may question the witness, but that's all."

Mr. Scharf turned back to Morris with a sigh.

"Aren't you ashamed, my son, that people spit in your eye when they hear your falsehoods?"

"I'm not lying. You might not want to hear what I say, but I'm telling the truth." Only his heightened color revealed Morris's anger. "Those who spit on me will be punished!"

He addressed Judge Korniss.

"Judge, Chief Recsky, Mr. Bary, Mr. Peczely, and Warden Henter will testify under oath they did not coach me."

"I'll ask you once more – has anyone ever threatened you or beat you to get you to testify falsely?" asked the judge.

"Never, sir! Nobody has ever threatened me or laid a finger on me!"

"Oh my son, what have they done to you?" cried Mr. Scharf. "I begged them to let you go. I even asked them at least ten times to give you Passover food during Pesach."

"I never wanted Passover food," said Morris. "I don't want to be a Jew any longer! I want to be Hungarian! My country will take care of me. Warden Henter showed me a letter from the Minister of Interior of Hungary that ordered him to look after me once the trial is over. The state will pay for my apprenticeship."

Mr. Scharf fell to his knees and began to beat his chest with his fists.

"I don't have a son anymore! My son is forever lost to me!"

Morris turned his back on his father.

"Stop your ravings, old man!" he said.

He looked a picture of calm until I noticed his fists were tightly clenched.

"I beseech you," cried Mr. Scharf, "tell the truth or they'll hang me! Won't you be sorry if they hang me?"

The boy stared at his father for an instance with eyes as dead as dark pebbles.

"If they hang you, it's not my fault," he said.

Mr. Scharf grabbed his arm, but he shook off his father's hand.

"Listen to me, Morris!" said Mr. Scharf. "If you don't tell the truth, they'll never let me go home!"

"They'll let you go! I made sure of that. They told me that if I . . ."

For one moment I thought that the old Morris, my friend, had reappeared. Then in an instant, he was gone again.

"What, Morris? What are you trying to say?" asked Mr. Scharf.

"Nothing! Nothing at all," the boy mumbled.

Mr. Scharf stepped closer to him, so that their faces almost touched. They had forgotten the people around them. They were alone in their misery.

"Look at me, Morris!" said Mr. Scharf. "Look at me and think carefully before you answer me. Why would the shochets, the ritual butchers, kill the poor girl?"

"It's a part of Jewish law that they needed her Christian virgin blood to make matzo."

"You know that's not true. It is ridiculous and you know it. For five thousand years we've abided by the Ten Commandments. 'Thou shall not kill.' Who taught you such things? Did you learn this in cheder?"

Morris shook his head.

"It's not a lie!" he cried. "Father Paul told me you do it. Father Paul would never lie to me!"

"You?" asked Mr. Scharf. "Why do you say 'you'? You are one of us!"

"No, I'm not!" said the boy. "Not anymore!"

Mr. Scharf collapsed to the floor, his hands over his ears against the dreadful words. Morris turned his back on him.

CHAPTER 22

TUESDAY, JULY 17, 1883

The carriage passed through the beautiful Tisza valley. The neat farms gave way to marshes and bogs that dotted the bank of the majestic river. A hawk soared high in the sky, a mere speck against the angry gray clouds ready to erupt any time. I didn't care. I burrowed into the cushions of Mr. Eotvos's carriage, enjoying every moment of luxury. When Mr. Eotvos had told me that he wanted me to travel with the court to Tisza-Eszlar, I didn't expect that Warden Henter would allow me to go. However, Mr. Eotvos spoke to the warden. I don't know what he said to him, but the warden gave his permission. I was surprised when I found out that I would be traveling with Mr. Eotvos himself. I was wearing a pair of stockings and leather shoes for the first time, both thanks to Teresa.

Our carriage wasn't the only one on the road. The entire court was on its way to examine the scene of the crime. When I stuck my head out of the window, I could see Warden Henter's carriage following us. Morris was traveling with the warden, Chief Recsky, Mr. Peczely, and Mr. Bary. The three judges' carriage came next. The defense attorneys were traveling with them. A horse-drawn cart occupied by the court stenographer and reporters covering the trial brought up the rear.

Mr. Eotvos was puffing on a fat cigar. Its sharp aroma tickled my nose. Mr. Heumann, the Jew lawyer who was the prisoners' first attorney, was sitting beside him.

Mr. Eotvos took the cigar out of his mouth and stared at me thoughtfully. I sat up straighter in my seat.

"I must confess, Julie, that I had ulterior motives when I invited you to travel with me," he said.

"I'm not that kind of a – !" The words escaped before I could stop them. I looked around the carriage for a place to hide.

Mr. Eotvos and Mr. Heumann burst into laughter.

"Don't be daft, girl," said Mr. Heumann.

"What do you think I am about, my dear?" asked Mr. Eotvos. "Why, I am old enough to be your father! It seems that I haven't been expressing myself properly. What I meant to say was that I wanted to talk to you and it would be easier to do so if we shared a carriage."

"I'm sorry, sir."

I could feel by the heat in my cheeks that I was blushing furiously.

"I noticed that you stopped attending the trial a few weeks ago after Morris's testimony. Many other people have testified since then," said Mr. Eotvos.

"It's hard for me to get away, sir, and Warden Henter doesn't like me to go."

"Julie, I am asking you to testify for our side. My clients have done no wrong. Their only crime is who they are – that they are Jews. Even in our parliament, there are rabble-rousers who speak against them. Several newspapers are accusing them of ritual murder. Ridiculous!"

He paused to puff on his cigar.

"I know, sir."

"I must prove my clients' innocence without the slightest doubt, and you, Julie, can help."

"Me, sir? I'm just a servant. Nobody would listen to me."

"I'll make them listen. I want you to recount in court exactly what you told me about the body the raftsmen fished out of the river. If we can prove that the dead girl is Esther Solymosi, my clients will be exonerated."

"Mr. Eotvos, I saw that body. I saw those clothes. It was Esther's body and they were Esther's clothes. I recognized her."

He took my hands between his.

"I believe you, Julie. In order to make the judges believe you, you must testify on the witness stand under oath."

All kinds of thoughts were running through my mind. Pa hated every Jew he had ever met, even Mr. Rosenberg who gave him the work that had put food on our table since I could remember. And Warden Henter – he warned me to stay away from the trial. I would lose my job when he found out I was testifying for the Jews.

I opened my mouth, on the verge of telling Mr. Eotvos that he would have to do without my testimony, when I recalled the desperation in Mr. Scharf's eyes. I thought of how they had made Morris ashamed of who he was. I no longer wondered about the right thing to do. I was certain. But I was too frightened to do it.

"Can I think about it, sir? It might mean my job. And my pa will have my hide when he finds out."

Mr. Eotvos took another puff of his cigar before answering. He tapped the ash out the window.

"Listen to me carefully," he said. "Doing the right thing is never easy. The Jews of Tisza-Eszlar and Morris himself are the victims of hate. Bary, Recsky, and Peczely are evil men. So is Henter. I know that it'll take tremendous courage on your part to tell the truth with them looking on in court, but I know you can do it."

"Please, sir. Let me think about it."

"Don't wait too long to decide," he said as the carriage slowed down and came to a stop. He looked out of the window.

"We've arrived," he said.

Word must have reached Tisza-Eszlar before we did because the street in front of the synagogue was packed with angry villagers. They were surrounded by a dozen gendarmes armed with rifles, bantering with them. There was no sign of Pa.

Their cries had become familiar to me. There were many versions of "Down with the Jews!" and "Killers!" and a forest of waving fists.

The gendarmes didn't seem concerned. They allowed them to vent their fury.

The synagogue was in an even worse state than when I had seen it. The yellow plaster walls were defaced with black paint and chunks were peeling away. We hurried inside. The dirty handprints were still all over the walls and the torn-up prayer books still lay on the floor along with all kinds of rotting garbage filling the building with a terrible stink. Every single one of the pews had been broken. I saw a rat scurry away along one of the filthy walls.

The Jewish prisoners were looking about with shocked and forlorn expressions.

"Mein Gott, what happened here?" Mr. Scharf picked up a book, its back broken, and cradled it in his hands. "Our beautiful shule. I always took such good care of it! Your Honor," he said to Judge Korniss, "let me clean up! Let me put everything back in its place. This is God's house."

Judge Korniss didn't bother answering him.

Morris was leaning against a wall with his eyes half-closed, twirling a closed umbrella in his hands. It was impossible to read his expression. I inched close to him.

"What's wrong with you? Stop lying!" I whispered urgently. He took a step away from me.

"I'm ready, Judge!" he announced in a loud voice.

All of us fell silent.

"Where did the murder of Esther Solymosi take place?" asked Judge Korniss.

Without hesitation, Morris led us into the covered, narrow passageway leading from the front door of the synagogue to the sanctuary. He stopped at the end of the hallway, in front of the entrance to the sanctuary.

"Here," he said, pointing his umbrella at a spot by the wall. "It's here that I saw Esther murdered."

"Are you certain?" asked Korniss.

"Yes, I am."

"Can you show us in which direction Esther was lying on the floor?"

Morris drew a large, rectangular shape on the dusty floor along the wall with the tip of his umbrella. Judge Korniss had two of the gendarmes place a straw-filled burlap sack inside the rectangle.

"This sack will represent the corpse," the judge announced.

"Esther's head was here," Morris said, tapping his umbrella at one end of the sack, "and her feet were here." He tapped at the opposite end. "Buxbaum was crouched down on the floor beside Esther over here." He used the umbrella like a pointer. "And Braun was beside him. Schwarcz was holding the pot here," he again pointed, "while he was cutting the girl's throat."

"Are you sure?" asked Judge Korniss.

"Yes, sir, I am."

"Let the court stenographer record the witness's testimony," ordered the judge.

The only sound was the scraping of pen against paper.

"I believe we're done here," announced Korniss. "Let's go outside. I would like the witness to re-enact what he did while the murder was taking place."

When the crowd of onlookers saw us, the gendarmes had difficulty restraining them.

"Silence!" cried the judge. The sure authority in his voice tamed the crowd.

"Morris," said Judge Korniss, "show us exactly what you did out here while Esther Solymosi was being murdered inside."

"I was peeking through the keyhole, Your Honor."

"You already told us that. Now, I want you to do exactly what you did on the day of the murder," repeated the judge.

Everyone was looking at the door, and everyone saw the same thing. The lock on the door was unusually low, at a height of no more than a half-meter off the ground. Morris's cocksure attitude wilted. He bent down to peek through the keyhole, but the keyhole was too low for him to look through. He had to drop to his knees onto the stone stoop to be able to look through it. And even when he was on his knees, he had to bend his neck into an awkward position to do so.

"This keyhole is lower down than I remember," he muttered. "The synagogue must have sunk lower down into the ground since I was here last. I was standing up before, while I was looking through the keyhole."

"It's impossible for the building to have sunk so far into the ground in fourteen or fifteen months that you have to get down on your knees to see through the keyhole if you didn't have to do that before," said Mr. Eotvos.

Morris flushed red but did not reply.

"How long did you look through the keyhole while you were observing the murder you described?" asked Mr. Eotvos.

"I already told you – three-quarters of an hour to an hour," said Morris.

He shifted from one knee to the other on the hard stoop, trying unsuccessfully to get more comfortable.

"I didn't hear you mention how tiring it must have been to remain on your knees with your neck twisted at an angle for the best part of an hour while you observed the crime through the keyhole."

The back of Morris's neck was splotched an angry red.

"You claim that the street on which the synagogue is located remained empty while you were on your knees looking through the keyhole, so that there was nobody you could ask for help," said Mr. Eotvos. "The street seems busy today."

"That well may be, but there was nobody here that day. And I told you I wasn't on my knees. The synagogue must have sunk!"

"My son, you're making a fool of yourself! Tell the truth!" Mr. Scharf shook his head.

"Mr. Scharf, be quiet!" Judge Korniss ordered.

"Morris, look through the keyhole! Can you see the burlap sack that represents the body?" asked Mr. Eotvos.

Morris put his eye to the keyhole and looked. Next he glared at Mr. Eotvos and then peered through the keyhole again.

"Can you see the burlap sack that represents the body of Esther Solymosi through the keyhole?" repeated Mr. Eotvos.

Morris mumbled something.

"I can't hear you, boy. What did you say?"

"I can't see the burlap sack," Morris said sheepishly, more loudly this time. "I might not see the sack now, but I did see Esther's body when I looked before!" He made me think of a cornered rat as he cast a frightened glance in Chief Recsky's direction.

The onlookers began to laugh.

"What do you mean you can't see the burlap sack?" asked the judge. "Get up! I want to look for myself."

Morris stood up and stretched his arms and neck.

Judge Korniss lowered himself to his knees with the aid of one of the deputies. He had to contort his neck in order to see through the keyhole.

"I can't see anything from here except an empty dark corner," he said. "What nonsense have you been telling the court, Morris?

"Let the court stenographer record that the location where the witness claims to have seen the murder is not visible through the keyhole!" said Judge Korniss.

All the learned gentlemen from the court were lowered to their knees to look through the keyhole. All of them came to the same conclusion. Morris's forehead gleamed with sweat as he tried to avoid looking at anyone.

Judge Korniss ordered the members of the court to return to Nyiregyhaza. At first I couldn't recognize the expression on Morris's face as he followed Chief Recsky and his colleagues to their carriage. Then I knew. It was fear.

I lagged behind for a moment. I dropped to my knees and looked through the keyhole. Judge Korniss was right. Nothing was visible except an empty dark corner of the covered passageway that led to the sanctuary. I could not see the burlap sack that represented my friend Esther's body.

It was late in the afternoon by the time I arrived back at the prison. Teresa was sitting at the scrubbed wooden table in the center of the kitchen. She had taken her boots off and had put her feet up on one of the chairs. A cup of tea was steaming in her hands despite the hot weather.

"I thought I would catch a few minutes of rest before starting on supper," she said. "Pour yourself a cup of tea. It's still hot."

I sat down beside her and we sipped the tea in companionable silence.

"Now tell me, what happened today?" she asked.

I told her how Morris's testimony had been discredited.

"Everybody could see that he was lying. Judge Korniss was angry."

"Can you blame him? It's time that boy unburdened himself in court and told the truth."

"I don't think that he knows what the truth is anymore." She put down her cup.

"The boy must be very frightened not to talk."

"Mr. Eotvos wants *me* to talk, Teresa."

I gulped down some of the hot tea, scalding my tongue and bringing tears to my eyes. Teresa ignored my distress.

"What does the lawyer want you to do?"

"He wants me to testify for the defense. If I do, Warden Henter is sure to fire me. And I can imagine how mad Pa will be. He doesn't care what's true or not. He just hates Jews. I don't know what to do."

She took the cup out of my hand, put it on the table, and grasped my fingers. The skin of her work-worn hands felt rough but at the same time so comforting.

"You know that I don't have much use for them Jews, Julie," she said, "but if Morris won't tell the truth, you'll have to. It's the right thing to do. If you don't testify, the Jews will end up in prison or worse. Could you live with that?"

I shook my head.

"Go find Mr. Eotvos," she said, "and tell him that you'll help him."

CHAPTER 23

THURSDAY, JULY 26, 1883

I tried to tidy myself as best I could the next morning. I washed my hands and face and a clean kerchief covered my hair. I had put my stiff new shoes on my feet and I even wore the embroidered blouse I reserved for church on Sundays.

It felt strange to be sitting on a bench with the other witnesses in the hall outside of the courtroom and not be skulking inside. Old Mrs. Csordas was on my right and Sophie Solymosi on my left. Sergeant Bako was standing next to us to prevent us from talking to one another.

A gendarme came out of the courtoom. My heart began to beat a rat-a-tat dance.

"It's your turn, Mrs. Csordas," he said.

I let out a sigh of relief. Mrs. Csordas, resembling an old crow in her black clothing, was escorted into the courtroom.

I was desperate to know what she had to say, but I was sure the judges wouldn't let me hear the other witnesses' testimonies. So I clutched my stomach and began to moan.

"I don't feel well, sir," I said to Bako. "I'm going to throw up my breakfast!"

He stopped tamping the tobacco in his pipe and looked up in alarm.

"Be gone with you!" He yanked me up from my seat. "Go outside! The fresh air will make you feel better." He pushed me in the direction of the staircase. "I'll come and get you when it's your turn."

I sped down the front steps and ran around the building to the side door. I slipped through it and then sat down on the floor behind my usual pillar. If I craned my neck around it, I could see and hear everything.

Mr. Eotvos ambled over to Mrs. Csordas and smiled in a friendly manner. Mrs. Csordas leaned back and responded with a toothless smile.

"I am the chief counsel for the defense," said Mr. Eotvos. "I'd like to ask you a few questions. How far is your house from the Jews' synagogue?"

"I'm only eight steps away from the Jew church, sir. I can see their front door from my windows."

"That's mighty close," said Mr. Eotvos. "I guess you are able to hear everything that goes on there."

"Yes, sir, I do. Them Jews can be mighty loud."

"As we all can be sometimes. Mrs. Csordas, you testified to Mr. Bary, the investigating magistrate, that you heard a child shouting in the synagogue during the afternoon Esther Solymosi disappeared. You said that these shouts seemed to be coming from underground. You also told Mr. Bary that the Jews left their synagogue later than usual on that day. They went home after twelve o'clock noon and not at eleven o'clock as on other Saturdays. Am I correct?"

"Yes, sir, that's what I told Mr. Bary, but I might have gotten my facts a smidgen wrong."

"What do you mean? You swore on the Holy Bible to tell the truth."

"I'm an old woman, sir. I was sick that day and my sickness addled my brain. I spent the whole day in bed. I didn't see when the Jews left their church. Later on in the evening, it was stuffy in my room, so I opened the window and I could hear a child's voice yelling in the Jews' church."

"Tell me, Mrs. Csordas, did this child's voice come from underground in the synagogue as you testified to Mr. Bary?"

The woman wrung her hands. "I'm not sure, sir. I'm an old lady."

Mr. Eotvos stepped closer to her. "Is it possible that this noise came from somewhere else, not from the synagogue, not from underground?"

"It could have, sir." She sighed in a pathetic manner.

The lawyer suppressed a smile. "So you are not certain where the noise came from?"

"No, I'm not."

"The noise you heard – are you sure that it was a child shouting?"

"I don't know . . . maybe."

"Ah, you're not sure of that either," Mr. Eotvos said, looking at the judges triumphantly. They stared back at him, their solemn expressions hiding their thoughts.

Mr. Eotvos was silent for a moment. He picked up a pencil from the defense table and began to tap it against his lips, as if he had forgotten about everyone around him. Mrs. Csordas squirmed nervously in her seat until he lowered the pencil.

"What time did you hear these noises?" he asked.

"I don't know exactly, sir, but it was already dusk."

Mr. Eotvos fixed his eyes on the judges again.

"Long after the alleged murder is supposed to have taken place," he declared.

He turned back to Mrs. Csordas and gave her a stern look.

"Now, Mrs. Csordas, listen to me, please."

"I am, sir."

"Did you look out of the window in your house that faces the synagogue between eleven o'clock in the morning and twelve noon on the day Esther Solymosi disappeared? Think carefully before answering."

"Yes, sir, I looked out of my window at that time."

"If you were so sick, why did you get out of your bed just to spy on your neighbors?"

"Oh no, sir! I wasn't spying! I had to go to the outhouse real bad, sir!"

The onlookers in the courtroom burst into laughter. Mr. Eotvos himself was biting his lip in order to maintain a solemn expression.

"Silence in the court!" Judge Korniss waved his gavel. "Silence or I'll clear the court!"

Reluctantly, everybody settled down. Mr. Eotvos turned back to the old woman.

"Mrs. Csordas, you're telling us that you looked out of your window facing the synagogue the morning Esther Solymosi disappeared?"

"Yes, sir, I did, on my way back from the outhouse."

"What time did this visit to the outhouse take place?"

"Ten or fifteen minutes before noon, sir. The sun was almost overhead."

"You're certain of this?"

"Yes, sir, I am."

"You looked out of your window at the synagogue at this time?"

"I already told you that I did, sir."

"What did you see?"

"Nothing, sir."

"What do you mean 'nothing'?" The folksy manner disappeared. Mr. Eotvos narrowed his eyes.

"Just what I said, sir. It was quiet. I couldn't hear their infernal Jew prayers. The Jews must have already gone home, sir. There wasn't a single one of them in sight. There was nobody about."

Mr. Eotvos let her words hang in the air. The onlookers sat expectantly, an audience at a play. Mr. Eotvos wheeled around to Morris.

"The witness Morris Scharf claims that he was standing in front of the synagogue door at the exact time you claim you were looking out your window. Morris states that he was looking through the keyhole of the lock on the synagogue door and observing the murder of Esther Solymosi inside the synagogue at this time. What do you have to say to that?"

"Nothing sir, because the boy wasn't there. There was nobody in front of the Jew church."

"Are you sure, Mrs. Csordas?"

"Yes, sir, I am. I'll swear on a stack of Bibles if you want me to. There was nobody standing in front of the Jew church. I might be old, but there is nothing wrong with my sight!" She crossed her arms across her chest and scowled.

The back of Morris's neck turned crimson, but he didn't look up.

"I'm sure your eyesight is just fine!" said Mr. Eotvos. "I have no more questions for Mrs. Csordas, Your Honor. I would like to call another witness."

Suddenly I forgot how to breathe. If I was next, Bako would discover that I wasn't waiting outside.

"I'd like to call Sophie Solymosi," said Mr. Eotvos.

Another reprieve. I began to breathe again. Mr. Szeyffert shot out of his chair.

"Your Honor," he addressed the judge, "Sophie Solymosi is a witness for the prosecution."

"The defense is aware of that," said Mr. Eotvos. "Nevertheless, we would like to ask the witness a few questions, Your Honor."

"Request granted," mumbled Judge Korniss.

One of the guards led Sophie into the courtroom.

"What is your name?" Mr. Eotvos asked.

Sophie adjusted her wide skirts over her knees and glanced at her mother before speaking.

"You know my name," she snapped.

"You must answer the defense counsel!" said Judge Korniss.

"I'm Sophie Solymosi."

"What was your relationship to the victim, Esther Solymosi?" Mr. Eotvos asked. I was struck by the gentleness of his manner.

"Esther was my sister," said Sophie.

She stared into the air, refusing to look at Mr. Eotvos. The silence in the courtroom was broken by Mrs. Solymosi's sobs.

"When did you last see your sister?" asked Mr. Eotvos.

"The day the Jews killed her!" cried Sophie.

"Your Honor, please instruct the witness to restrict her responses to answering my questions," said Mr. Eotvos.

"Answer Mr. Eotvos's questions, girl, but keep your opinions to yourself," said the judge.

"So the last time you saw your sister was the day she disappeared, correct?" asked Mr. Eotvos.

"Yes."

"Where did you see her?"

"Rosie Rosenberg and I were out walking. We met Esther by the Tisza River."

"What time did you meet her?"

"It must have been about one o'clock in the afternoon."

"Are you sure of the time?"

"Yes, sir. We left the Rosenbergs at half past the hour, after we ate our lunch, and must have been walking for at least a half-hour."

Mr. Eotvos scratched his chin.

"That's strange," he said in a perplexed voice. "Morris Scharf testified that he witnessed your sister's murder between eleven o'clock and just before noon on that day."

"I don't care what Morris says. I saw my sister and she was still alive at one o'clock!"

"How was your sister dressed the last time you saw her?"

"I don't remember," mumbled Sophie.

"Judge, please remind the witness she must answer my questions," said Mr. Eotvos. "You must tell the truth in court, Sophie," he added gently.

"Esther wore a red shawl, a white apron and blouse, black skirt and a red, white, and black plaid jacket. She also had her red-striped belt around her waist. She always said it was the prettiest thing she owned."

"Did she have shoes on?"

"No, although it was very cold for April, she was barefoot. She was freezing, but Mrs. Huri wouldn't let her wear her boots."

"Did Esther have anything in her hand?"

Sophie looked at the judge. "Do I have to tell him?" she asked.

"Answer him," said Judge Korniss.

"She was holding a small tin container. I asked her what was in it. She told me it was powdered paint she bought at Kohlmayer's."

Mr. Eotvos stepped closer to her.

"I am sorry, but I must ask you a few questions that might be painful to you."

"What do you mean?"

"What was your sister's mood when you saw her? Did she seem happy?"

"No."

"How do you know that she wasn't happy?"

Sophie pleated and unpleated a fold of her skirt.

"She was crying," she said so quietly I had to strain to hear her. "She told me how mean Mrs. Huri was to her and how unhappy she was. She said she didn't know how much longer she could go on."

"That's a lie!" a voice came from the back of the room. It was the unmistakable squawk of Mrs. Huri. "I was always kind to the lazy little witch!"

"Silence!" thundered the judge.

"I told Esther that Mama was trying to find another job for her and then I left her!" cried Sophie. She covered her face with her hands. "I should have stayed with her when I saw how upset she was. I shouldn't have let her go!"

Mr. Eotvos handed his handkerchief to her. She balled it in her fist.

"The Jews killed Esther," she said. "Esther may have been crying, but the Jews killed her. I just know it!"

"The Jews should hang for what they did to my sister!" Janos Solymosi, his arm around his mother's shoulders, called out. "They should burn in hell for what they did!"

"Be quiet or I'll have you removed from the courtroom," said Judge Korniss.

"I have no more questions for this witness," Mr. Eotvos said.

"I suggest we finish for today," said the judge. "Do you have any other witnesses?"

"Yes, sir," said Mr. Eotvos. "I would like Julie Vamosi, a friend of the victim, to testify tomorrow."

"We'll start with Julie Vamosi's testimony tomorrow morning, ten o'clock sharp," Judge Korniss said.

I ran back to the hall in front of the courtroom as fast as I could. Bako was pacing back and forth.

"You took long enough!" he said. "I was about to come for you!"

I was saved from having to reply by the doors bursting open and the onlookers streaming out of the courtroom.

"Go home, now," Bako ordered, "but be sure that you're here by ten o'clock tomorrow morning!"

That evening, I knelt by my bed to say my prayers. Though I was exhausted, I couldn't sleep. I kept thinking about Ma and Clara and how much I missed them. I hoped that Ma was happy in heaven.

"Take care of Clara, Ma, until I can look after her," I whispered. "And, Ma, please, help us to be together again."

I thought of Morris and his father and decided to put in a good word for them too.

"Ma, please watch out for Morris and his papa. They've suffered so much!"

Once again, for a brief moment, I felt as if Ma was in the room with me. I saw the gentleness in her eyes and I felt the love in her heart. I put my hand out to touch her, but she disappeared. I drifted off to sleep.

The next thing I knew somebody was shaking my shoulders. I sat up groggily and wiped my eyes. Pa was standing by my bed. Warden Henter was beside him.

"I'm off now, Vamosi!" said the warden. "Remember! I didn't see you today nor do I know anything about what's going on here. Keep the noise down!"

The bars of my cell clicked shut behind him.

I could smell the liquor on Pa's breath. I pulled the blanket closer around my shoulders.

"Warden Henter tells me you want to testify tomorrow. Now why would a daughter of mine help those people?"

"I only want to tell the truth, Pa!"

"What are you going to say?"

I shrunk farther away from him.

"The truth, Pa," I repeated. "I want to tell the truth."

"You don't know the truth!" His voice echoed off the plaster walls until the room was full of his words.

He picked up the wooden boxes that served as my table and chair and smashed them on the floor. Splinters of wood were everywhere. For a fleeting moment I remembered the broken pews in the synagogue in Tisza-Eszlar.

"Truth! What do you mean by the truth?" Spittle pooled in the corners of his mouth "It's bad enough that my mates laugh at me because I have to work for that damned Jew Rosenberg, and that we've had to take their wretched charity. Now my daughter wants everybody to know she is a Jew lover! I wouldn't be able to show my face around town!"

I shut my eyes.

"Listen to me carefully!" The quiet of his voice only made his words more menacing. "You will say nothing!"

"But, Pa . . ."

The sting of his slap silenced me. He yanked my hair to pull me upright and began to pummel me with his fists. I tried to shield my face with my hands but to no avail. The front of my shift was stained red, so I knew my nose was bleeding.

"What are you going to say in court?" He shook me like a rag doll.

"Mr. Eotvos told me to tell the truth, Pa, about how I identified the corpse that was fished out of the river. The dead girl was Esther for sure. I recognized her."

He dropped me back onto the cot.

"Now listen to me carefully! You will say no such thing to the judges. You will tell them you have never set eyes on the dead girl before!"

He grabbed hold of my shift and pulled on it roughly, then let go. I rolled off the cot, my pillow falling down beside me. The cot tipped over. Pa and I saw it at the same instant: my small hoard of coins wrapped in cloth. I reached for it, but Pa's hand clamped down on my wrist so I dropped the precious bundle. He scooped it up.

"What have we here?" he chuckled, putting it into his pocket.

"Pa, please! It's money I've been saving so Clara can come and live with me. Pa, she's miserable at Aunt Irma's. Ma would want us to be together!"

"Your ma wouldn't want you thieving from me!" He pulled me off the floor roughly and began to squeeze my throat. I tried to pry his fingers off my neck with no success. His fingers tightened. Black spots appeared in front of my eyes. Suddenly, he let go and I fell back to the floor, gasping for air.

"Now listen!" he cried. "You better do as I tell you or you'll regret it! Tell the judges tomorrow that you never saw the dead girl before!"

With a last kick to my stomach, he was gone. I waited for a few minutes before I tried to move my arms and legs. Nothing seemed to be broken but everything hurt. I sat up with a great deal of difficulty. It took me a moment to realize that the ragged sound I was hearing came from my own throat.

I crawled back to my cot and righted it. I lay down, my mind a jumble of fears. What should I say in court tomorrow? I knew Pa always fulfilled his threats. What could I do to get my money back? "Please, Ma, please, Ma, help me!" I prayed. I listened, willing her to come back, but I couldn't find Ma again.

CHAPTER 24

FRIDAY, JULY 27, 1883

For the rest of the night the demons in my brain were as bad as the pain in my body. I relived every blow from Pa's hand, every sneer that distorted his face, and every foul curse that escaped his lips. I could have borne it if he hadn't taken the money from me. Clara would die of neglect, thinking I'd deserted her if I couldn't take care of her myself. And unless the day had more hours, I could not work harder or longer. The constant work and hardships were worth it if I could make a home for Clara. But otherwise? I couldn't bear it any longer.

I closed my eyes and conjured up the time when Esther and I were still young girls in short skirts. When Ma was alive and Pa didn't drink. When the only thing we knew about Mrs. Huri was that she had shiny wooden floors in her house and that she gave generously when the collection plate was passed in church. I realized that those carefree little girls lived only in my memory in a time that was always summer and the days felt as if they would never end.

I stared at the cracks in the plaster walls that ran like a river across the room. I remembered Esther, hidden in the bulrushes, safe for the moment from Mrs. Huri's sharp tongue. I finally understood what she was trying to tell me the last time I saw her by the village well. I hated the thought. Surely she would not have done that to herself! I crossed myself quickly. I couldn't say the word *suicide* even to myself. It was a mortal sin that condemned you to eternal damnation! Yet, it was the only rational explanation of her death, but I couldn't bear to believe it, not if it meant that Esther's suffering would go on through eternity. Somehow I had to convince myself she was murdered by the Jews. But I knew well that the Jews were innocent.

How could I betray Esther? The shame it would bring her family! She would even be denied her final resting place in the hallowed grounds of a Christian cemetery. I felt as if a knife had stabbed me through the heart.

I lay on my cot hour after hour, waiting for the terrible night to be over. I was afraid to move because even the smallest motion caused terrible pain. My left eye was swollen shut, but I could still see the moonbeams streaking the clay floor of my cell. When dawn stole into the room through the bars of the window high up on the wall, I pulled myself up to sit, catching my breath before I lowered my feet to the ground. The pain was so intense I had to bite my lips not to cry out loud. An evil spirit seemed to have passed through my cell. My meager furnishings were broken into pieces and thrown about as if they were pieces of kindling. I tried to stand but fell back down to the cot. The agony in my stomach and legs was overwhelming. It took several excruciating tries before I was finally on my feet. I pulled on my skirt and my Sunday blouse gingerly. My kerchief was still missing. I finally found it on the floor in a corner of the cell next to Ma's workbox. It was upended, with all of her needles and yarns littering the floor.

I was bent over and clutching my stomach as I made my way through the empty hallway to the kitchen. Although my cell was just a few meters away, it took me several minutes to get there. Teresa must have gone to the market because the kitchen was empty. She'd left the shutters open to catch the breeze and cool the hot kitchen for the day's cooking. I poured some water from a pitcher into a basin and washed myself as best I could. My stomach heaved when I saw that the water was turning pink. I decided that I would worry about cleaning it up later.

I cut myself a crust of bread to gnaw on. Every mouthful hurt. I forced myself to eat. I knew I would need my strength. I ran my fingers over my lips. They were twice their normal size. I wished I owned a looking glass so I could see my face. I tied my kerchief under my chin and pulled it as far forward as I possibly could to cover my face. It was time for me to go.

The streets were already swarming with men making deliveries of food, maids off to market for the day's provisions, and visitors who had tickets for the trial and wanted to get an early start on the lineup for seats. I must have presented a frightening sight. People either stared at me with horrified expressions or quickly averted their eyes as I slowly shuffled past them.

I thought I should use the same entrance as everyone else when I arrived at the courthouse, so I walked up the broad public staircase. Every step hurt. Bako was waiting for me. His eyes rested on my battered face, but he said nothing as he led me into the courtoom. I passed Pa, who was sitting next to the door.

"Remember what I told you," he whispered. I didn't respond. He had become, and would always be, a stranger to me.

The judges were already at their table.

"Ah! Your witness is finally here, Mr. Eotvos. About time!" said Judge Korniss.

His mouth fell open when he took a closer look at me. The onlookers in the courtroom began to whisper among themselves.

"What happened to you?" asked the judge.

"I had an accident, sir."

"Are you all right, Julie? Is there anything you want to tell me?"

Mr. Eotvos's voice was full of concern.

"I'm fine, sir. I fell down."

I could see by his expression he didn't believe me.

"Are you able to testify? You can return another time if it's too painful today."

"I'd like to get it over with, sir."

"If you're quite sure . . ."

"I am, sir."

I was glad of my swollen eyes. They gave me the excuse I needed not to have to meet his gaze. The court clerk swore me in.

"Tell the court your name, please," Mr. Eotvos said.

"I'm Julie Vamosi."

"What was your relationship to the victim, Esther Solymosi?"

"She was a good friend, sir."

"How well did you know her?"

"As if she were my own sister. We used to play together every day when we were young girls. After we grew and she went into service, and I had my chickens and my eggs, we were together every hour we could steal."

"I must ask you a few questions that might be difficult for you," said Mr. Eotvos. I braced myself.

"Do you remember what happened on Monday, June 19, 1882?"

"How could I forget? That was the day when a group of rafters fished the body of a dead girl out of the Tisza River at Csonkafuzes. It was an awful sight. Mr. Bary was there, as well as Esther's mother and sister and brother."

"What happened then?"

"Mr. Bary asked Esther's family and two or three of their relatives from Tisza-Eszlar to look at the dead girl. When they finished, he asked me to look at her too."

"What did these people say about the dead girl? Did they think she was Esther Solymosi?"

"No, sir, none of them thought that . . . not even Mrs. Solymosi. All of them were positive it wasn't Esther's body."

"What about you? Did you think the dead girl was Esther?"

The moment I had dreaded had arrived. The courtroom fell silent. All eyes were on me. Nobody noticed Pa rising out of his seat in the back row and glaring at me with burning eyes. Nor did they see the hardness of Bary's face as he looked at me or the anger of Recsky's expression. I tasted fear in the bitterness of my mouth and felt it in the clamminess of my hands and in the cramping of my stomach.

"I'm sorry, Mr. Eotvos. I'm so sorry, but the body was in such a terrible state – bloated and buffeted by the waters – that I couldn't be sure if she was Esther."

A tightening of his lips was the only sign of the shock Mr. Eotvos must have felt. Pa gave me a mean smirk and sat down.

"Are you sure, Julie, that you can't identify the dead girl as Esther Solymosi?" asked Mr. Eotvos.

"I'm sorry, sir, but I can't."

I kept my eyes on the floor because I couldn't bear to look into his eyes.

"I have no more questions for this witness," Mr. Eotvos said to Judge Korniss.

"Witness dismissed," said the judge. "You may step down."

As I rose from the witness chair, I happened to glance at Morris. His eyes were dull with hopelessness in his white face. I could do nothing about the injustice of Esther's short and hard life and her death, or her mother's sorrow, or the sickness that claimed my own dear ma, or Aunt Irma's cruelty to a helpless child. I couldn't make the man who fathered me treat me like a human, much less his daughter. In that moment, I realized that here was an injustice I could right. I realized I didn't have to add to the sum of misery. I heard the judge's words as if he were calling from a great distance.

"I told you that you may sit down."

I did. I sank back into the witness chair once again.

"Your Honors, I'd like to change my testimony because the testimony I just gave is a lie."

"Consider your words carefully, girl," barked Judge Korniss. "Do you want us to put you in jail for perjury?"

"I'm sorry, sir . . . so very sorry," I said, looking at Mr. Eotvos. "I didn't tell the truth before because I was so afraid."

I untied my kerchief and gave the judges a full view of my battered face. The noise level in the courtroom became deafening. Judge Korniss hammered the felt-covered table with his gavel.

"Does your fear have anything to do with your injuries?" Judge Korniss sounded kinder than I'd ever heard him.

"Yes. My pa beat me up."

Pa cried out, "You lying bitch!" A guard tried to restrain him. Pa swung at him and missed, then swung again and the guard doubled over.

"Take that man into custody! I will not tolerate such a disruption."

"She's my daughter, ain't she? I can do with her whatever I want." Pa's words were barely coherent. He fumbled in his pocket for his flask.

Judge Korniss spoke a word or two to the judges flanking him and stood up.

"Deputies," he said to the armed guards by the door, "take that man into custody. We will deal with him later."

The noise in the courtroom grew even louder as everyone scrambled for a look at the deputies as they grabbed hold of Pa's arms and snapped handcuffs over his wrists.

"You'll pay for this, bitch! You will pay!"

The deputies dragged him out of the courtroom. The onlookers sat down

"Mr. Eotvos, continue your cross-examination of the witness," said the judge.

"Julie, please tell the court again what happened on the banks of the Tisza River near the town of Csonkafuzes on Monday, June 19, 1882."

"It all started when a group of Jewish rafters floating down the Tisza fished a dead body out of the river, sir. By the time I got there, Mr. Bary and several other gentlemen from the city were standing around the body of a dead girl. I already told the court that Esther's mother and sister and brother were also there, as well as some of their friends and relatives from our hometown of Tisza-Eszlar."

"Were there any Jews from Tisza-Eszlar present at the time?"

"No, sir."

"Go on."

"Mr. Bary asked Mrs. Solymosi and Sophie and Janos to identify the dead girl. They insisted it wasn't Esther. All of this happened before I got there."

"What happened after you arrived?"

"Mr. Bary asked me to look at the poor girl."

"And?"

"I did what he told me to do, sir. I looked at her very carefully."

A great sadness overwhelmed me as I recalled the poor wretch's bloated body and ravaged face. I covered my mouth for a moment.

"It was just awful to see what the water did to that girl."

Mr. Eotvos looked toward the judges as if to check that they were paying attention before asking his next question.

"Did you recognize the corpse?"

"I did, sir."

Chaos erupted in the courtroom.

"Silence!" cried Judge Korniss as he banged his gavel. "Silence!"

"Who was the corpse? Whose body did Mr. Bary ask you to identify?" asked Mr. Eotvos.

I paused for a moment to compose my answer because I wanted my response to be crystal clear.

"The dead girl was Esther, sir. She was my friend Esther Solymosi."

"Are you certain?"

"Yes, I am."

"What did Mr. Bary say when you identified the corpse as Esther Solymosi?"

"He told me I was wrong." I raised my voice slightly to make my point. "I wasn't wrong! I'm certain that the poor dead girl was Esther!"

"How can you be so sure, Julie? Even the victim's mother insists the corpse was not her daughter."

"I recognized her! Despite the way she looked, I could still see Esther's features beneath all the damage done to her face by the river."

"Liar!" cried Mrs. Solymosi, jumping up from her seat. "Shut your mouth, you liar! That ugly lump was not my beautiful girl!" Her pain was as fresh as it had been that day on the riverbank.

"She was Esther!" I told her. "You just don't want to admit it because of what the river did to her!"

"Please sit down, Mrs. Solymosi," said Judge Korniss. "Sit down or I'll have you removed from the courtroom!"

He turned to me.

"You will only answer questions from the defense counsel! Understood?"

"Yes, sir. I'm sorry, sir."

"Let's continue with our cross-examination," said Mr. Eotvos. "Julie, you claim you recognized the corpse Mr. Bary asked you to identify?"

"Yes, sir, I did. She was Esther, but there were also other reasons why I knew it had to be her."

"What reasons?" Mr. Eotvos asked.

"The girl was naked as the day she was born when Mr. Bary told me to look at her. However, the clothes she was wearing when they found her were lying on the ground next to her. They were the same clothes I saw Esther wearing the last time I saw her alive, the day she disappeared."

As I shifted on my chair, my bruised body protested and I almost yelped from pain. I tried to find a more comfortable position.

"Sorry, sir, I need a moment to catch my breath," I told Mr. Eotvos.

"Are you all right? We can continue tomorrow."

"I'm fine, sir, just sore."

He poured water into a glass from a jug on the defense table and handed it to me. It helped a little.

"I'm fine now, sir. I can answer your questions again."

"All right, let's proceed. You claim that first you identified the corpse as your friend Esther Solymosi and then you recognized her clothes. What clothes were there?"

"A red, white, and black plaid jacket, a red-striped belt, a black skirt, a white apron and blouse, and a white under-skirt were lying on the ground beside Esther. A tin box was on top of the clothes. She had the same container in her hand the last time I saw her alive. She needed it for the paint she was going to buy at Kohlmayer's."

"Are you sure?"

"I am, sir."

"Are you certain she was wearing the same clothes the last time you saw her alive?"

"Yes, sir. I am."

"So let me repeat again. You identified the corpse as being Esther and the clothes as belonging to her. And there was also the container for the paint you saw before."

"Yes, sir."

"What makes you so sure you weren't making a mistake?" he asked.

He looked around the audience to gauge their reactions. I followed his gaze. Everybody was hanging on our every word.

"I recognized Esther and her clothes sir, but there was also her scar."

"Scar? What scar?" Mr. Eotvos looked astonished.

"When we were young, Esther tried to milk her cow, Magda. The cow trampled on Esther's right foot. Ever since, there was a large crescent-shaped scar at the base of her right toe. I must have seen it a thousand times. The body from the Tisza had the same scar at the base of her right toe."

"Are you sure about this?" asked Mr. Eotvos. "I read the report of the pathologist who examined the corpse and there was no mention of a scar in it!"

"The girl is telling the truth!" cried a voice from the left side of the courtroom and a man in city clothes stood up. It took me a moment to recognize him. He was one of the men who had been standing around Esther's body on the bank of the Tisza River. I remembered him because he had told Bary not to be so certain the Jews had killed Esther.

"Silence, Zuranyi!" cried Judge Korniss. "What are you thinking, interrupting court proceedings like this?"

"I have to, Your Honor. I have no other recourse. I saw the scar on the victim's foot myself. I asked Bary why the scar wasn't mentioned in the report made by the pathologist. His response was that I should mind my own business."

"Is that true, Mr. Bary?" asked Judge Korniss.

Bary rose from his seat.

"Your Honor, the pathologist who examined the corpse did say that there was a faint scar at the base of the dead girl's toe. I didn't think this was significant-enough information to include in the report, so I told him to leave it out."

"Well, you were wrong, sir!" roared the judge. "It's not your job to decide what's important and what's not. Mr. Szeyffert," he said to the prosecutor, "you better confer with your clients about what other evidence they might have excluded from their records."

"I will, Your Honor," Szeyffert said. His heightened color betrayed his embarrassment. "I will make sure nothing like this will happen again!"

The judge nodded his head regally. "Continue with your cross-examination," he said to Mr. Eotvos.

By now, my legs were cramping from sitting so long, but I forced myself to remain motionless.

"So, Julie," said Mr. Eotvos. "Forgive me for repeating myself, but you are giving us very important information. You recognized the corpse the raftsmen fished out of the Tisza as being Esther. You testified that the clothes piled up on the ground beside the body were Esther's clothes, and you talked about the scar at the base of Esther's toe and the corpse's toe. Correct?"

"Yes, sir."

"Now, think carefully before you answer me. What did the victim's neck look like?"

"What do you mean, sir?"

"What kind of mark did you see on the throat of the corpse fished out of the Tisza?"

Memories of what was left of that ravaged body brought bile to my mouth. I swallowed hard.

"There was nothing on Esther's throat, sir . . . not a single mark. And I could see her neck clearly because the poor girl was naked."

"Do you mean to tell me there was no cut or scar on the throat of the corpse?"

Sadness overwhelmed me. Not only did my friend lose her life, she had even lost her name.

"Mr. Eotvos, could you please not refer to Esther as 'the corpse'? She was a person. She was my friend. She had a name."

Mr. Eotvos tapped his finger against his lips.

"You're right." he said. "I would like to apologize and rephrase my question. Did you see any marks or cuts on the throat of your friend Esther Solymosi?"

"No, sir. There wasn't a single mark on Esther's throat," I repeated.

I was conscious of the shuffling feet and stirring bodies around me.

"You're telling us, Julie Vamosi, that the victim, Esther Solymosi, had no cut or scar on her throat?" asked Mr. Eotvos.

"Yes, sir, that's exactly what I'm saying."

"My clients," said Mr. Eotvos, dramatically pointing to the prisoners' bench, "are accused of cutting the throat of Esther Solymosi and draining her blood into a pot. How could they have done this if there was no cut or scar on the girl's neck?"

"They couldn't have, sir."

I kept my eyes on Mr. Eotvos so I sensed, rather than saw, several men scrambling to their feet and shaking their fists at me. I forced myself to look at them. As much as my swollen eyes and lips would allow, I tried to look dignified and defiant. "I do not believe the Jews killed her!"

I heard Judge Korniss's gavel just as Mr. Szeyffert jumped up from his seat.

"Your Honor, please instruct the witness to keep her opinions to herself!"

"Just answer what you're asked," the judge told me.

Morris had not moved during the commotion. He sat with head hanging down and his hands tightly clasped together between his knees.

After several moments, with some help from the armed guards, the judge managed to restore order in the courtroom.

"I have just one more question for you," Mr. Eotvos said. "You and Esther were friends for a long time, so you must have known her well."

"Yes, sir. I did."

"How was Esther feeling the last time you saw her? What was her mood like?"

My eyes burned with tears. How much should I tell him? Then I made up my mind. I would not sacrifice the living for the sake of the dead. Mr. Eotvos was entitled to know. "Forgive me," I said to Esther before answering the lawyer.

"Esther and I always had a good time together. She was always ready for a lark, but she changed after she started to work for Mrs. Huri. She used to be like a songbird, singing all the time, but then she didn't sing anymore. She didn't even seem to care about the mean things that Mrs. Huri said, or about having to work every hour that the Good Lord sent. When I saw her that last time, on the day she disappeared, she was miserable, cold, and hungry. I'm worried that she found her life so hard, too hard, that she might have. . . ."

I had to stop speaking because my unshed tears were choking me.

"What were you going to say?" asked Mr. Eotvos. "That Esther might do what?"

"Nothing, sir. I was just rambling on."

I could not express what I feared the most, because sometimes when we say out loud what we fear, our fears become reality.

—

CHAPTER 25

MONDAY, JULY 30, 1883

I had left Teresa to cook, serve, and clean up breakfast through much of the trial, and though she grumbled about it, I knew she was willing to do all the work in return for a daily first-hand update. But on Monday she was feeling poorly and I stayed to help her, over her loud and vulgar protestation. I didn't get to the courthouse until just after Mr. Szeyffert finished his summation of the case. The sweltering courtroom was half empty and I had no trouble finding a seat among the men. My eyes scanned the room anxiously for any sign of Pa before I remembered he was locked up. I let out a sigh of relief when I realized he wouldn't be able to hurt me again. Bary, Peczely, Recsky, and Henter, looking limp in the heat, were sitting beside each other. You can't hurt me either, I exulted. Once again, Morris had the front row to himself.

"Why is the courtroom so empty?" I asked a lad in simple country clothes next to me. "I would have thought it would be bursting at the seams on the day the lawyers give their final summations." I wiped the sweat trickling off my brow with the edge of my apron. "Everybody must be staying at home because of the heat!"

"It's not that," said the boy, looking me over boldly from head to toe and bringing a blush to my cheeks. "After that lying Jew boy's testimony, people are saying that the murdering Jews will get off. Who wants to see that?"

A man in the row in front of us turned around.

"Don't be so sure of an acquittal, my friend!" he cried. "Everybody knows that the Jews killed that poor girl. I'll wager you that the Jews will hang at the end of a rope before long, just like they deserve!" He held up a shiny new coin.

"I'll bet you they won't!" It was one of the men who worked on Mr. Rosenberg's farm.

"The Crown will now call upon the defense for its summation," announced Judge Korniss.

Mr. Eotvos stood up from the defense table. He seemed at ease and was smiling.

"Your Honors," he said to the three judges, "as counselor for the defense, it is usually incumbent upon me to prove to the court the innocence of my clients. However, I do not have to do that in this case, for the facts here speak for themselves and demonstrate that the defendants are not guilty.

"These defendants," he continued, gesturing at the prisoners, "are accused of the ridiculous charge of ritual murder. This charge is based upon ignorance. One may have expected to see such foolishness in the Middle Ages, but it is shocking in our modern times. Investigating Magistrate Bary did not allow truth to stand in his way. He decided at the outset of this case that the accused were guilty and he twisted the truth to support his suppositions. The prosecution's case rests upon Investigating Magistrate Bary's imagination."

Bary jumped up. "How dare you!"

Judge Korniss sounded impatient. "Sit down, Mr. Bary! I'll handle this!"

The courtroom was humming, except for Morris, who remained still as death.

"Be careful of what you say, Counselor! You are dangerously close to defamation of character!" bellowed Judge Korniss.

"I am sorry, Your Honor," answered Mr. Eotvos. "I was carried away by the heat of the moment."

"Continue, Mr. Eotvos," said the judge, "but I would like to see more moderation, please."

"Yes, Your Honor," Mr. Eotvos said, a half-smile on his lips. He faced the audience. "Ah, where were we . . . ? Let's start at the beginning, when Esther Solymosi disappeared. After Esther disappeared, Morris Scharf was one of the suspects. When Mr. Bary realized that the prattle of five-year-old

Sam Scharf would not stand up in court, Morris suddenly became his star witness. Morris's testimony was full of inconsistencies and lies."

Morris did not react to Mr. Eotvos's words. He was a statue, his hands clasped in his lap, his head lowered as if he was in prayer. The gentle rise and fall of his chest was the only sign he gave of being alive.

Mr. Eotvos paused for an instant before beginning to speak again.

"I would like to note here that Morris was separated from his family and indoctrinated against them and his fellow Jews. As a result, he suffers from moral blindness."

He turned back to the judges.

"Your Honors, let me summarize for you Morris Scharf's claims.

"Morris stated that on the first of April, in the year of Our Lord 1882, between the hours of eleven o'clock in the morning and twelve noon, he was standing in front of the door of the synagogue in Tisza-Eszlar. He said that he was peeking through the keyhole of the lock located on the aforementioned door. He claims that he saw through the keyhole the ritual murder of Esther Solymosi by my clients, Schwarcz, Buxbaum, and Braun, after Herman Vollner led her into the synagogue.

"Please let the court note that when he was asked what part of the body of the victim defendant Braun was holding down while he was allegedly restraining the girl, he had difficulty answering this question.

"Also, when he was asked if the blood of the victim gushed out from her neck or was a mere trickle, he said the blood trickled out of the girl's neck, then changed his mind and replied that the blood gushed out of her neck like a geyser.

"Thirdly, Mrs. Stephen Csordas, who lives next door to the synagogue in Tisza-Eszlar, recounted the testimony she had given to the investigating magistrate. She is no longer certain that she had heard a child's voice coming from underground in the synagogue. She now believes that she may have heard "noises" coming from somewhere else in the evening, long after the alleged murder is supposed to have taken place.

"Furthermore, Mrs. Csordas is able to see the front entrance of the synagogue from her windows. She looked through her windows at the front door of the synagogue between eleven o'clock in the morning and twelve noon on April 1, 1882. This was the exact time and date that Morris Scharf maintains he was standing in front of the door leading into the synagogue and was peeking through the keyhole of the lock of that door. He claims that he saw the ritual murder of Esther Solymosi by my clients. Mrs. Csordas testified under oath that she did not see Morris Scharf standing in front of the synagogue door and looking through the keyhole at this time, on this date. She insists that Morris Scharf was not in front of the synagogue at this time, on this date, regardless of what he claims.

"And finally, Morris Scharf's credibility was completely destroyed during the court's visit to the Tisza-Eszlar synagogue. I won't even speak of the location of the keyhole, that it was much closer to the ground than the witness had stated. However, I will speak of the witness's field of vision through the keyhole. As we have heard repeatedly, Morris Scharf stated that he looked through the keyhole of the lock on the synagogue door. As Your Honors yourselves have observed when you looked through the keyhole, all you could see was a dark corner of the passageway connecting the entrance of the synagogue to the sanctuary. You couldn't see the spot where Morris claimed the murder had taken place!

"It is self-evident, Your Honors," continued Mr. Eotvos, "that the testimony of Morris Scharf should be disregarded!"

The judges stared back at Mr. Eotvos impassively. Morris kept his eyes on the floor.

I could hear people moving about to see better, but nobody spoke. The prisoners were nodding their heads. Mr. Scharf was weeping.

"Furthermore, I would like to remind Your Honors that the witness Morris Scharf claims to have observed the ritual murder of Esther Solymosi between eleven o'clock in the morning and twelve noon on April 1, 1882," said Mr. Eotvos. "However, the victim's sister, Sophie Solymosi, stated unequivocally, under oath, that she saw her sister alive at one o'clock in the afternoon on that date. How could Esther have been killed by my clients between the hours of eleven and noon as claimed by the witness for the prosecution and then rejoin the ranks of the living at one o'clock in the afternoon? The answer is simple – she couldn't have. Therefore, Morris's testimony has been proven to be false again!"

He looked around the courtroom. The hostility of the onlookers toward him was almost palpable.

"How much longer are you going to take, Counselor?" interrupted Judge Korniss. "You made your point already."

"I must respectfully state, Your Honor, that I am entitled under our penal code to defend my clients to the best of my ability. That is what I am doing," said Mr. Eotvos in a pleasant voice.

Judge Korniss glared at him but didn't reply.

"Where were we . . ." said Mr. Eotvos. "Ah, yes, my proving my clients' innocence . . . and that brings us to the problem of the corpse of the young woman fished out of the Tisza River near the town of Csonkafuzes. Was this corpse the body of Esther Solymosi? Mr. Bary maintains that the Jews dressed the body of a strange girl in Esther Solymosi's clothes."

He paced in front of the railing dividing the judges from the rest of the courtroom.

"I would like to prove to the court that the corpse was the body of Esther Solymosi," he finally said. "First of all, Julie Vamosi, the victim's friend, recognized the dead girl as Esther Solymosi."

I could feel people looking at me when he spoke my name. I sunk lower down in my seat and pretended I was invisible.

"We mustn't forget," said Mr. Eotvos, "that the corpse fished out of the river was wearing the same clothing as Esther Solymosi the day she had disappeared." He walked over to the defense table and picked up a thick sheaf of paper. "Although it was not revealed through witness testimony, these court records state that there were two nails in the pocket of the victim's apron." He waved the document in the air. "Court records also show Mrs. Csordas asked the victim to buy nails for her at Kohlmayer's. We have also established through witness testimony that the victim was clutching a container of blue powdered paint in her hand. Esther is known to have purchased paint of this color on the day she disappeared. There was also the matter of a large crescent-shaped scar at the base of the victim's right large toe. Interestingly, no mention was made of this scar in any official reports."

He turned toward the judges.

"Your Honors, it is evident that the defense has proven without any reasonable doubt that the corpse at Csonkafuzes was Esther Solymosi!"

Several people in the audience began to boo. Mr. Eotvos waited until they stopped.

"Mr. Bary does not want to admit that the Csonkafuzes corpse was Esther Solymosi because the throat of the dead girl did not have a single blemish on it – not a cut, not a scar," he said. "My clients are accused of cutting Esther Solymosi's throat. How could they have done so if there wasn't a single mark on it? The answer is simple – my clients did not cut Esther Solymosi's throat. My clients are innocent!"

Pandemonium broke out in the courtroom. Judge Korniss had abandoned his gavel and was shouting for order. Mr. Eotvos was the center of the storm. He stood, hands clasped behind his back, waiting for the noise to subside enough for him to be heard. When he began to speak, the courtroom fell silent.

"We must now consider the final question: if my clients did not kill Esther Solymosi, and we can see that they did not – who did?"

With measured steps, he walked over to the defense table and poured himself a glass of water. The courtroom was so quiet I could hear him swallow as he drained his glass. "We'll never know to a certainty what happened to Esther Solymosi, but may I suggest that perhaps the poor girl found her life under a demanding mistress so difficult she might have taken matters into her own hands?"

The only sound was Mrs. Solymosi's moan as Mr. Eotvos returned to his seat. For the first time since Mr. Eotvos began his summation, Morris raised his head. I couldn't stand to look at the agony in his face.

Judge Korniss stood up. "My esteemed colleagues and I will examine the facts of this case in chambers. We will return a verdict as to the innocence or guilt of the defendants in due course. You may be sure that justice will be done."

I was not so sure. By the expressions on the faces of the defendants, I could see that they shared my uncertainty.

—

CHAPTER 26

FRIDAY, AUGUST 3, 1883

I was on my hands and knees, scrubbing the slate floor of the kitchen, when two sturdy boots blocked my way. I looked up at their owner. A man in a peasant's pantaloons and embroidered vest towered over me. He drew a pouch out of his pocket, took a pinch of tobacco, and began to chew while I struggled to my feet. I wiped my hands on my apron.

"What do you want?"

He spat tobacco on my clean floor. I bit my lip to dam the angry words that were fighting to escape.

"I'm looking for Julie Vamosi," he said.

"I'm Julie."

"Mr. Eotvos asked me to fetch you. He said to tell you to come to the courthouse right away. The judges are about to give the verdict." With a quick nod, he was gone before I could tell him to clean up his gob of tobacco.

"I'm off, Teresa," I called into the courtyard where she was shucking a pile of corn.

"Mind you remember every single detail for me." She grinned in anticipation. I took off my apron and smoothed down my hair. Cleaning the floor would have to wait.

The street in front of the courthouse was swarming with people. It looked like market day, except the whole city was covered by leaflets that reminded me of white snow. Even the trees had leaflets attached to them. Almost every house was plastered with posters. A woman stood in front of one of them, reading it aloud to the little boy holding her hand: "It says that we're supposed to remain calm." He laughed at the cartoon of a man with a hooked nose and long forelocks.

I wedged myself into the sweating crowd in the courtroom and tried to breathe despite the stench of unwashed bodies and cologne. Journalists, pads open and pencils poised, stood by the entrance. The door to the ladies' section was wide open and it was packed too. I elbowed my way to the pillar in front of the side door. At least, it afforded me protection on one side.

I could see the prisoners from where I stood. They looked terrified. Mr. Eotvos moved from one to the other.

I think he was trying to reassure them because as he passed, each of them looked at him gratefully. Solomon Schwarcz swayed in his seat, his eyes closed and his lips moving in prayer. Mr. Scharf was speaking to Lipot Braun, and for a moment the two men squeezed each other's hands. Only Morris, in his regular spot in the front row, was motionless. He seemed unaware of the clamor around him.

The clock on the wall chimed eleven times. The door of the judges' chamber swung open and Judge Korniss and his two colleagues entered. I tried to read their expressions. They did not look at the prisoners.

Judge Korniss began to read a long document that described all the charges that were laid and all the testimonies that were made during the trial. He concluded by stating that the testimony of the witness of the Crown, Morris Scharf, was questionable and therefore the charge of murder against Solomon Schwarcz, Lipot Braun, Abraham Buxbaum, and Herman Vollner was not proven beyond reasonable doubt, nor was the charge of complicity to murder against Joseph Scharf.

I waited for the judge to declare the defendants not guilty, but the declaration did not come. The journalists were scribbling furiously.

Mrs. Solymosi's cries that had underscored the whole trial rose once more. "Punish the Jews!"

Sophie wept by her mother's side and Janos shook his fist at the defendants. When I turned toward the doors, the journalists were all gone.

I expected celebration from the prisoners, but it didn't come. They looked relieved but exhausted too. There was a sadness about them I couldn't begin to understand. Mr. Eotvos, Mr. Heumann, and their colleagues shook hands with them all. When they got to Mr. Scharf, he pointed at his son. Mr. Eotvos said something to him and Scharf sat down.

Nobody wanted to leave the courtroom and they didn't want to let the prisoners go. I could hear cries of "Shame!" and "Hang them!"

I saw Recsky jump up and start shouting at the judges. Henter and Peczely were pulling on his arms, trying to get him to sit down. Bary was beside them, shaking his head in disbelief.

Armed gendarmes surrounded the prisoners to protect them. The man beside me had climbed up on his chair for a better view. He used my shoulder for balance as he got down.

"I don't understand. Were the defendants acquitted? Is the judge saying they are not guilty?" I asked him.

"The damn Jews won the case! It's a shame, but all of them will go free."

In the midst of the confusion, noise, and heat, Morris sat bewildered. Everybody seemed to have forgotten about him. I started to make my way toward him, but a tide of people pushing toward the exit carried me away.

I was walking down the front steps of the courthouse when somebody tapped me on the shoulder. It was Mr. Heumann, smiling ear to ear.

"What a day!" he cried. "I have a message for you from Mr. Eotvos. He asked me to tell you to come to his chambers this afternoon. He is staying at the Hotel Central. Be there at four o'clock. I'll be waiting for you in the lobby."

He dived back into the crowd before I could ask him any questions.

—

CHAPTER 27

FRIDAY, AUGUST 3, 1883

At first, Teresa was worried. "What are we going to do when Henter gets back? He's going to blame you, you know, and you'll be out on the streets. What's more, I'll be without a scullery maid."

"I'll ask Mr. Eotvos's advice. He wants to see me this afternoon."

"In his hotel room?" Teresa gave me a lewd wink, but I ignored it. Instead, I gave her a moment-to-moment account of everything that had happened. She clucked at the verdict, but she had no time for Bary or Henter or the others and was happy they had lost. She had me describe their disappointed expressions over and over while I peeled four buckets of potatoes and cut up five dozen onions for the prisoners' dinner.

Then she had me wipe my hands on a metal pot to get the onion smell off and she helped me tie my hair back with a white ribbon. I changed into my Sunday blouse and set off for the Hotel Central.

The hotel was not far from the prison, but I made slow progress. I had never seen so many people in one place before. I flattened myself against a wall to make way for a band of angry men clutching clubs in their hands.

The Hotel Central was on the same street as the Nyiregyhaza synagogue. I wondered if the freed men had gone there. Suddenly, the wooden door of the synagogue flew open, almost knocking me over. Two men in long black coats and black hats stepped out. They immediately ducked back into the building when a rock flew in their direction. That's when I noticed the arsenal of rocks across the street and the jeering young men ready to throw them. I ducked past them.

I was out of breath and my heart was thumping loudly as I ran up the hill to the Hotel Central. A man in a fancy uniform guarded the entrance.

"Where do you think you're going, wench?" He was not impressed by my blouse or my new white hair ribbon. "Take your hide to the servants' door at the back!"

"I'm sorry, sir, but I was told to meet somebody in the lobby."

"What's the matter?" It was Mr. Heumann. "Is there a problem? I was waiting for this young woman to arrive."

The guard's manner underwent a miraculous transformation.

"Of course, sir, of course. I was just about to take this young person to you."

Mr. Heumann held out his hand to me. The lobby, with its paintings on the wall, its thick carpet, and its enormous velvet-covered chairs, dazzled me.

"Come . . . Mr. Eotvos is waiting for us," he said.

I tore my eyes away from the gilded ceiling and followed him up the wide staircase. Mr. Heumann rapped on one of the doors that lined the long corridor.

"Come on in. It's open."

"I'll leave you now," said Mr. Heumann. "Mr. Eotvos wants to speak to you in private."

Mr. Eotvos was in an armchair. Across from him sat Morris. Mr. Eotvos stood up when he saw me, but Morris just turned his face away.

"Thank you for coming, Julie," said Mr. Eotvos.

"I'm glad to be here, sir, but I saw terrible things in the streets on my way here."

"As soon as the verdict was announced, demonstrations against the Jews started." He sighed. "Let's hope they'll blow over quickly.

"You must be wondering why I wanted you to come here. First of all, I wanted to thank you for your help. It took a lot of courage on your part to testify. I was also hoping that my young friend here" – he looked at Morris –

"will talk to you. He won't speak to me or to anybody else. His parents will be arriving momentarily."

I walked over to the boy. "Hello, Morris."

He didn't look at me, nor did he respond.

"Morris, say hello to Julie," Mr. Eotvos said.

"It's me, Julie. Talk to me!"

Morris was so still that for a moment I wondered whether he had heard me. I looked at the lawyer, who shrugged his shoulders.

I circled Morris's chair so that I was directly in front of him. His eyes were dull and empty. I crouched down beside him and took his hand. He tried to pull it away, but I held it tight.

"You told me I was your only friend, Morris. You thanked me for remaining loyal to you despite my doubts. Do you remember?"

He nodded slowly, as if the movement hurt him. "I understand what happened. You have to figure out a way to keep going." If I thought that his misery would bring Esther back or erase the way he'd made innocent people suffer, I would have been happy to let him suffer too. But I knew that nothing could be undone.

His face crumpled.

"Oh, Julie, what have I done? What have I done? I am so sorry! I was so wrong," he sobbed, "but they kept on telling me that . . ." The stream of excuses was cut off by the sudden loud knocking on the door. Mr. Scharf stood on the threshold. Mrs. Scharf, holding Sam by the hand, was behind him. Morris recoiled, but Mr. Scharf opened his arms wide.

"My son," he said, "my son!"

Morris dropped to his knees in front of his father. Mr. Scharf tried to lift him up. Morris grabbed his father's hand and kissed it.

"Papa," he said, "please, Papa, please . . . forgive me!"

—

CHAPTER 28

SATURDAY, AUGUST, 4, 1883

"How much longer, sir? How much longer?" I asked Mr. Eotvos.

"We'll be there soon. A half-hour at the most."

"How can I ever thank you, sir?"

He leaned back against the seat of the carriage, puffing on his ever-present cigar.

"No need to thank me. Just work hard."

"I will, sir."

How I wished that fancy words came more easily to me because I so much wanted to tell him that I would not disappoint him. I wanted to tell him that he would not be wasting his money by paying for my apprenticeship with a dressmaker in Budapest. That had been Ma's dream for me. He had even offered me the use of a small flat in his home during my training. I would have room and board and I would help the housekeeper for pocket money.

The carriage drew to a stop in front of the dreary farmhouse. A child dressed in rags was scattering corn to a gaggle of geese in the yard. She looked up at the sound of the carriage. It was Clara.